Some of These Days...

Christopher Kerr

Michael Terence
Publishing

First published in paperback by
Michael Terence Publishing in 2020
www.mtp.agency

ISBN 9781913653316

For Jessamy, Polly and Gemma.

FOREWORD

Over a period of ten weeks in the late summer and early autumn of 1970 a series of messages appeared in the personal column of The Times. They seemed to be more or less unsuccessful attempts to set up a number of rendezvous with a hostile if unidentified organisation in the Middle East. There was a suspicion of hostage-taking. A central figure went by the code name Q.

What were they?

A spoof to advertise a spy book or film? It was, after all, the time when James Bond was in his prime.

Or was it a subtle plug for a holiday company?

For a new aftershave?

But it might have been something more serious: it was also a time when tensions were higher than usual in the Eastern Mediterranean. The Six Day War was not long in the past. In September Leila Khaled of the Popular Front for the Liberation of Palestine attempted to hijack an El Al flight from Amsterdam to New York. Hijackings became for a time almost a common event.

Readers turning eagerly to the back page of The Times each day hoping for the next instalment or an explanation were, in the end, disappointed. The messages ended as abruptly as they had begun.

Others may long ago have solved the mystery but, if so, I never heard the truth. This, using the messages as a framework, is a not wholly serious guess.

ONE

AUGUST 10, MONDAY
BEIRUT

> George in Beirut. Meeting fixed Beau Rivage Hotel
> 4.15 10 August. Woman in red carrying Times. Q.

George Spofforth sat alone at a table in the Beau Rivage hotel, Beirut. He was fortyish, fattish, and florid. He was not, he knew – that is when he bothered to think about it – a distinguished-looking man; nothing was further from the cinema's notion of the Brylcreemed lounge lizards who, in the matinee idol tradition, are the habitués of Middle Eastern hotel bars. His once thick fair hair was receding now and, although his appearance was not a great concern of his, he was happier to let it go from the front where he could keep an eye on it, rather than on top where the shining pate might creep up on him in an unexpectedly-positioned mirror. He glanced at the empty glass in front of him and waved a waiter across. "Bring us the bill, old scout, would you?"

***

If you wrapped your arm around one of the metal uprights by the train's door and used it as an anchor, gripping your Times in both hands, it was possible to achieve some kind of lateral stability. With luck you could read as many as five words at a time before you were jolted off balance and the paper jerked from your line of vision. Since the press of other passengers didn't allow the possibility of turning a page, you had to choose a particularly promising page before you got on and hope that it provided material to last your journey. The back page of the Times, with its personal column recently removed from the front when the Times fell into line with other papers and began, rather self-consciously, to put news there, was ideal. In those two central columns lay tiny histories, jewel-like cries for help, microcosms of life: career-moves, flat-shares, sits vac, anything legal considered, each a self-contained perfection in ten words. No need to struggle to remember what you had been reading at the moment your elbow was jogged; each time it was a new start, a fresh story, a different discovery.

$$***$$

AUGUST 19 1970
LIVERPOOL

Andrew Wilkinson pushed his way out of the newsagents, turning at once to the back page of his Times. He wove his way through the early morning crowd trying unsuccessfully to read the small print as he walked. When he reached the little station in Mersey Road he folded the paper in four and began to study it more carefully. He didn't at first find what he was looking for and, having read the two columns, he went back to the start, running his finger line by line down the page.

Towards lunchtime, Steve Bolland put his head round Andrew's door.

"Not a lot, no." Andrew was saying into the phone. "We haven't discussed that part, that element of the problem. Well, as soon as we can, I'm due to see him this afternoon, but you – you know how these things can slide."

Steve pointed to his watch and made drinking motions. Andrew shook his head. "Shopping," he mouthed.

"Technically speaking, you're absolutely right," he went on. No, no, I'm assuming nothing. Sorry? No, not a human – assuming. Quite right. Right. Fine. Yes. Okay. Okay, Goodbye. Good. Goodbye."

He hung up, smiling to himself. "Interesting thought," he said quietly. He picked up the phone again and dialled a number. It rang for a long time. In due course he hung up again and went out.

Over the last week, in his usual cursory skim through the personal column, Andrew had noticed what seemed to be a series of messages. This was unusual. Sometimes a lover would respond to a lover, sometimes an advertisement would string itself out over a day or so but, in general, Andrew assumed, people sent their replies to the box numbers provided. Correspondence in the column itself seldom went on for more than a day or two. However, so far he had identified five entries which clearly made up a series of related messages. In his flat the previous evening he had looked through the pile of last week's papers by his bin and had torn out entries which seemed relevant from the days before. A visit to the library at lunchtime and a scan through the back numbers had confirmed that they seemed to start, quite abruptly, without preamble, on **August 7**.

"George in Beirut", it read, "Meeting fixed Beau Rivage Hotel 4.15 10 August. Woman in red carrying Times. Q."

The others ran, in sequence:

August 8

George in Beirut. Refix Beau Rivage meeting midday 10 August. Contact as before.

Then there was a gap until **August 13** when:

Q. August 10 meeting failure due limpet. Refix alternative contact/location. George.

August 14

George in Beirut. Le Vendome Hotel bar 17 August 11pm. Peter in horn-rims. Recognition seven. Q.

This was the one which had first caught his eye; hadn't there, he thought, been something about George in the day before? From then on he had scanned the column each morning for the next instalment.

August 18

Q. George missing. Commodore room ransacked – radio gone. Le Vendome contact 17 August failed. Instructions? Peter.

That had been yesterday's. It was followed today by:

Q. Enforced departure Beirut. Arrived Istanbul, staying Hilton using passport five. New contact/ location urgent.

George.

It was intriguing stuff. What was it, a clever plug for a new book, an immensely complicated love affair, industrial espionage, or perhaps just someone having a laugh?

He stretched and dialled the number he had tried earlier. After a few rings it was answered.

"Hi, it's Andrew," he said. "Are you back?"

"Got back last night."

"How was it?"

"Wonderful."

"Free for a drink tomorrow?"

"OK."

"Sevenish? The Adelphi?"

"All right."

"See you tomorrow then."

Andrew put the phone down and turned back to the papers. He read the first one out loud:

"George in Beirut. Meeting fixed Beau Rivage Hotel 4.15 10 August. Woman in red carrying Times. Q."

"My train was late this morning," said Andrew after the waiter had unloaded their drinks.

They had met in the cocktail bar at the Adelphi. Andrew liked its shabby opulence and the informal attentiveness of the waiters.

"It arrived late and it managed to lose time as we went along. I began to think there was a conspiracy. All the signals were red, there were people digging up the track every three miles, every station was crowded with old ladies who could only get on or off with enormous difficulty. Well you know how I hate being late and having to explain every bloody time. I sat there and cursed the whole railway system, the hopeless bloody railmen, the rotten clapped-out trains and before I knew it we'd stopped again, right out in the middle of nowhere halfway across Chat Moss, you know, where all those chimneys are and the factories choking up the canal with that brown froth. I was so angry I couldn't work, couldn't even read the paper. Then, as we moved off again, I heard these two blokes further down the carriage. Apparently there'd been a body on the line. They'd seen the police van. They thought someone had fallen off a bridge. And, do you know, it was suddenly all right again. I had a genuine reason for being late and it wasn't anybody's fault and besides I had a cracking story to tell. That poor sod, by conveniently – well not for him I suppose – falling on to the track, had saved my day."

"Was he dead?" Lesley asked. "I think so, yes." He had a drink. "So that was a bright start to the day," he went on breezily. And now here I am with you." He looked expansively round the empty bar. What could be better?"

"What indeed?"

"It was your hair."

They had sat, after the party not at this table, but in a corner, very close to each other with the excited conspiratorial closeness of people who might be about to become lovers. They had been talking about Eddie Cochran.

"Of course I remember him," she had said. "I'm older

than you think. It's this hair."

She had touched her hair cursorily as one might half-stroke a troublesome cat. Her hair was long, you might say too long for her age. When she released it from the rubber band that held it, it reached her upper arms. But it was the thickness of it that somehow made it unusual. Hair of that length is generally fine and well-combed and straight; hers was combed but it had a liveliness which set it apart. It was not hair through which you ran your fingers, it was hair which you weighed in your hands, warm, with a subtle wave, and heavy. It went with the half-smile, the distant sparkle in the eye, the rare, longed-for hand on his arm. Together they seemed to be contriving a double-bluff. "We seem mature, but we are young. Yet not so young."

"How old are you anyway?" he had asked.

"Why do you want to know?"

"Just interested. I want to know all about you."

"No, you want to stick me in a box. You want to see how much younger I am – if I am younger, you don't know."

"Why are you so sensitive about your age?"

"Aren't you? Of course you are. Think about it; our ages always define us. I bet your parents used to say things like 'isn't he bright for his age?' or 'he was an early reader'. There's this huge pressure to achieve – and the younger the better. You've got to get there first. So, suppose I tell you I'm twenty-four?"

"Are you?"

"I'm not saying. Suppose I am? What's your reaction?"

"I don't know."

"Liar. You're thinking 'she's probably lying but I don't

want to offend her by suggesting she looks older than she is'."

He smiled. "Not bad, Gypsy Petulengro."

"You see? It can become such an issue. Don't worry about how old I am – or you are, I don't need to know. Just think of me and you."

"Okay. Fair enough." He touched her hair with the back of his hand. "It's really thick, isn't it? And warm. And kind of rich."

"You make it sound like gravy."

They had both laughed and he moved to kiss her. She shifted slightly so that his cheek was against hers and he was looking over her shoulder. A girl had been sitting at a table at the far end of the cocktail bar. She was wearing well-cut red trousers. That was all that Andrew had been able to see of her because the rest was hidden behind the copy of the Times which she was reading.

"I much prefer it short," Lesley was saying. "It was so much trouble before."

Andrew stared at her and glanced back at the table where the girl in red had been sitting. It was empty.

"Oh well," he said. "Autre temps autre moeurs."

"Plus ou moins," she said.

It would start, he supposed, with a scene where George, whoever he was, would pick up one of the early messages in the Times personal column…

AUGUST 10, MONDAY
BEIRUT

George glanced at the empty glass in front of him and waved a waiter across. "Bring us the bill, old scout, would you?" He took his wallet from his pocket and pulled out some folding money. A small newspaper cutting fell out and floated to the floor and he grovelled grumbling to pick it up. He put it on the table. It was an entry from the small ads of the Times, heavily ringed in red biro.

The waiter came back with George's bill and fiddled on his tray with change.

"This is the only bar in the Beau Rivage, isn't it?" George asked him.

"Yes, sir. There is sometimes little bar in dining room when we have dance but that does not happen very much now."

"I can imagine. So, if I were meeting someone in the bar, this would be it?"

"Yes sir, I think so. I don't think we have seen you before at the Beau Rivage?"

"Good God no, I normally drink at the El Shamir. This is a bit upmarket for me."

The waiter handed him his change; George put some coins back on the tray.

"There you are, old boy," he said cheerfully. "By the way. Do you get English newspapers here?"

"Some, sir. Daily Mail, Times, Herald Tribune."

"That's not English for Christ's sake; it's barely human. Don't tell me you've grown up here without knowing the difference between an Englishman and a Yank? Has the

Times come in yet? Must be about due."

"I will go and ask, sir."

George picked up the scrap of newsprint and stared at it.

"Woman in red, eh? That makes a change. Do with a bit of totty in this business. Chance would be a fine thing. Bound to ask me questions I can't answer just to make certain I know she's my intellectual superior. Perhaps I'll just smile winningly and say I prefer girls on top. Or not. Oh, well done, lad!"

He watched the waiter approach with a copy of the Times. George reached in his pocket and handed him some coins.

"Good show. Have a smoke on me." He laid his finger along his nose and winked. The waiter smiled, bowed and went. George glanced at the headlines but, after a second or so, turned to the back page which he read attentively.

"Bugger," he said heavily after a moment or so. "Why can't they get anything right? Who wants to meet at bloody midday? Don't they know anything?"

He stumped out of the hotel lobby and into the harsh Beirut sunlight.

Is this really going to work? Andrew asked himself. Is it really plausible that a spy, if that's what George is, is going to communicate through the Times personals? Surely that's a bit cumbersome, not to mention extremely public? Why not a radio? Well perhaps because radios are themselves cumbersome, have a limited range and are fairly easy to intercept. Perhaps the point is that, as long as they talk in code, there was no need to hide the messages; wasn't here something about recognition seven? And the great thing about this method was that you only had to send it once –

other agents could keep in touch with events wherever they were. The only thing was that you had to plan a bit ahead, allowing time for the papers to be delivered. But this usually only took a day, so perhaps it wasn't such a bad system. Well it must be all right because the real George, whoever he was, was certainly using it. Let's stick with it for the moment. He had no real idea what Beirut looked like; he wondered whether it and Liverpool had anything in common beyond their derelict buildings and bomb-sites. He tried to imagine Lime Street with palm trees and passers-by in burnouses.

George blinked in the bright sunlight. He bellowed at a taxi which, after a moment's hesitation, swerved suddenly left and began to fight its way across the lanes of traffic It arrived beside him, panting slightly like a willing dog. George got in.

"The Haj Belem baths, old fruit. Good God, talk about the insolence of office. Those bloody pen-pushers, I bet they just changed the time for something to do."

From the steamy darkness of the Haj Belem other bathers heard the continuation of George's long complaint. Through the echoing seediness he could be made out sitting on a stone slab in a sweating alcove, wrapped in a towel. From time to time one of the bathers would pause at the entrance to the alcove and listen, uncomprehending but respectful to the steady flow of grievance. On the other side of the alcove Tom Prendergast sat, equally courteously listening. George railed at the inefficiency of British bureaucrats and their habit of hiding themselves behind a smokescreen of codes. The point of the bureaucrat, he assumed, was to convince you that he is vital to the smooth running of whatever operation he was currently buggering up. But this secrecy made George suspicious and, he insisted to Tom, if they made you suspicious it meant that he couldn't be doing his job very well, could he? And so why, he was bound to ask, was it necessary to change a meeting?

The towelled figure who had been listening discreetly beyond the alcove moved silently away as if he knew that there was no answer. Just round the corner another pair of feet paused to listen.

What was wrong with 4.15, George wanted to know, and what was so special about mid bloody day?

The bare brown feet padded off into the steam.

If this were a film, there would be a clever dissolve here from the steam in the Haj Belem to the steam which was rising from the shower, misting the curtain. Andrew stopped typing and rested his head on his hands, remembering.

Behind the curtain moved the outline of a figure, perhaps two. A glance below it revealed two pairs of feet standing close together in the confines of the cubicle. In its damp intimacy Andrew ran his hands over Lesley's slippery back, his mouth against her ear.

"It's heavier when it's wet. It must weigh pounds. Doesn't it make your neck stiff?"

"I've probably developed good neck muscles."

"I think all your muscles are outstanding."

"Do you like muscles?" she asked.

"I like yours."

"So do I."

Andrew opened his eyes and rolled another sheet into his typewriter. He needed to move things along.

George was staring moodily out of the taxi's window at the cheerful mayhem of the El Akbar. Beirut was an endearingly European city with its pavement cafés and elegant women. You might have thought Nice or San Remo but for the weight of the heat; it was not the crisp sunshine of the Western Mediterranean but the leaden furnace of the desert. Since it was nearly noon the street was comparatively quiet as shops began to close and business people prepared for lunch and the siesta. And he had to have a meeting. George's disgruntlement had lessened only slightly.

The driver had looked hard into his mirror once or twice.

"Excuse if I ask one question, sir?"

"Fire ahead, old son."

"You are meeting friends at the Beau Rivage?"

"Yes, I suppose so."

"You meet them there?"

"That's it," said George in the tone of patronising testiness one uses to an importunate child.

"They know where to go, yes?"

"I assume so. Why do you ask?"

"Because car behind drive very close behind. I think he

follow us. I wondering if it your friends who don't know way to Beau Rivage?"

George turned to look out of the back window.

"You are expecting to be followed perhaps?"

"No, not at all. I can't imagine who they are."

"No problem. I lose them." said the driver, changing down two gears.

"No, don't worry," said George, grabbing the back of the driver's seat. "Just take it easy."

The taxi drew up abruptly on the forecourt of the Beau Rivage. It looked very like the Adelphi except that the pillars were white marble and the doorman wore a flowing burnous and ornately-gilded headgear.

"Would you wait, old fruit?" George asked the taxi-driver as he got out carrying a small package.

He walked fast into the foyer, followed at a short distance by a man in a blue suit but without a tie who had got out of the car behind. George went briskly to the lifts and got into one just as the doors closed. Two other men were already in it. The man in the suit raced up the stairs to the first floor and stood by the lift-gate. When the lift did not stop he ran up to the second floor. Fortunately for George it was a fast lift and he had by now reached the fourth floor. The other passengers got out and George pressed the G button. His pursuer reached the fourth-floor landing just as the doors closed and found it empty. He ran up another flight of stairs. George's lift meanwhile reached the ground floor again; he crossed the lobby and walked briskly out to the waiting taxi.

"The Commodore please, old chap," he said.

As he drove off the driver of the car which had pulled in behind him, got out and ran inside. He found his sweating colleague stumbling down the stairs into the lobby. As they stared around them in angry bewilderment they did not notice, over by the swing-door, a dark-haired girl in a white blouse and red skirt staring seriously at George's retreating taxi. In her hand she carried a copy of the Times.

The first time he saw Lesley she had been wearing that same skirt. They had stood close together, not touching, at the edge of the not-dim-enough room. She was looking at him as she talked swiftly and quietly; he replied from time to time, slowly and looking at the floor or at her hands or at the wall; his eyes had seldom met hers.

He supposed that it had been on the cards that they would end up together. Both had, it turned out, come to the party alone, knowing few people, had introduced themselves to each other and had recognised the similarity of their situations. It was this that had kept them talking to each other; it was better than the awkward side by side silences or the solitary studiedly-casual drinking and watching on the fringe.

He imagined that he would dance with her a bit, take her home, kiss her and, without conviction, take it from there. But that was up to her. He felt no urge to do so beyond a stray remnant of a young man's pride, a sense of achievement and the blessed, undemanding comfort of strangers. Presumably the same thoughts were forming in her subconscious somewhere behind the soft, endless ribbon of words which came from her. The artifice of their companionship heightened his sense of remoteness; he didn't want her, didn't particularly care for her and yet was reluctant to leave her. She had, when all was said and done, a sweet half-smile, astonishing luxuriant hair and she had, even if for her own purposes, done him the honour of staying with him throughout the evening. He would have been jealous if she had moved away. She didn't, but continued to talk with quiet, affectionate energy. It was almost as if she was afraid that it was he who would move away.

That evening George sat comfortably at a table in the El Shamir bar leafing through a paperback. Opposite him sat Tom Prendergast. Tall, bald and sixtyish, he stared out into the room with the vague and faintly querulous gaze of the man well past his third double. He swung his head with unnecessary vigour towards George as George put the book rather too loudly down on the table.

"It's no good," said George, "I can't find it. Been that sort of day. Anyway it's a bloody good bit of writing. Catches the mood of the place perfectly. I'll put a marker in the page when I find it. You ought to read it."

"Love to," said Tom winningly. "My trouble is I don't get a lot of time for reading these days. Just a quick flick through the old paper and that's about it."

"I hate the bloody papers. Give me a good novel any time. Papers haven't got anything in them except war and crime and bloody politics and strikes and all that crap. I don't want to be reminded what a lousy world I live in. You're much better off in fiction."

As he spoke he had the faintest impression of having remembered some piece of unfinished business; he could not however pin it down and swirled the straw-coloured wine round his glass. The good thing about Tom was that he was a good listener, fundamentally polite and supportive in the way of Shaw's Colonel Pickering. Not given to difficult questions, he was happy to sit back, half-dreaming, half-listening to George's flow, content in the knowledge that things weren't what they were when he was a lad.

Deep within George, by contrast, lay a seam of unrequited rancour, directed fairly specifically at the futility of ambition, the absurdity of hope, the farce of work. Those Victorians had known what they were doing when they invented the work ethic and the sanctification of other people's labour. The object of the exercise, to borrow his platoon sergeant's favourite phrase, was to keep the worker from feeling that he knows what he's doing. The security of the manager, George realised, lay in the perpetual precariousness of the pawn.

Tom leaned forward confidentially, trying to speak with great clarity.

"I've got to go up to the old wadi tomorrow to look over a new vineyard. Strictly in the line of business of course. If it's any good I might be in for a few hectolitres, for the locals anyway. Why don't you come? Thought you might be interested in shipping some of it. What do you say? We could be up there by opening time."

AUGUST 12, WEDNESDAY
LONDON

Q's office was large, well-furnished along senior civil-servant lines: a reasonable carpet, heavy reproduction desk and chairs, small Turneresque prints of Amalfi and Naples on the wall as well as (Q had both taste and good connections) a small oil by Howard Hodgkin he'd picked up at a Chelsea Art School show; decanter and glasses on a side-table. Q was standing staring at a large map of the Middle East when there was a knock at the door.

"Come in," he said and Tenison entered. Tenison, Q's immediate deputy, was in his thirties with straight ginger hair and tortoiseshell glasses which were probably the same ones that he had worn at school. He was one of those men who had never been so happy as when they were at school, and his wide-eyed eagerness to please had certainly, Q thought, been forged in the ruthless struggle to survive at some godforsaken boarding school, perhaps in the Midlands. Tenison, who even now had the look of a junior prefect, had survived by being keen. He was the one who always asked questions, was always first with his hand up, who always laughed loudest at the master's jokes.

Nor had he managed to lose his taste for infantile jokes. Far from having outgrown the adolescent penchant for sexual jokes, he had hardly reached it. What made him laugh were jokes about lavatories and bums. Q thought that, while undoubtedly intelligent, Tenison had, on balance, reached his level; advance into the subtler forms of the higher diplomacy did not seem imminent.

"Hello, Alec," he said. "Any news from the Times?"

"Not a squeak. We've got monitors on all the telex and cable wires but there's nothing through and no reason to suspect bad transmission."

"Bloody little man," said Q quietly. "What the hell's he playing at? All he has to do is pass on a simple message. Can't he even manage that?"

He moved over to his desk and idly tidied some piles of paper.

"I think we should give him more time," said Tenison. "He may be trying now for all we know. We don't know what conditions are like out there. After all he's never been late before, has he?"

"Not being late is not the same thing as being perfectly reliable, Alec. It's always going to be touch and go with George. You can never be certain he's going to make it."

"But he always has."

"So far. But that doesn't stop me from having the nasty feeling that he won't next time. His record has a feeling of unreliability about it. It's a feeling I'm getting increasingly just now, aggravated by the even nastier sense that this time I'm going to be right. And, let's face it, he gives no sense of understanding what he's doing."

"He hasn't. That's why you picked him."

"I didn't pick the man; the service wished him on me."

"But you didn't object. You thought, if I remember, that it would be rather useful to have an agent working for us who would never reveal anything to an enemy because he had nothing to reveal. And who was so simple that he would genuinely never wonder why he was required to make the occasional rendezvous and send slightly puzzling messages back to the people he thinks are importing his wine. 'A man without curiosity' I seem to remember your saying, 'the perfect cypher'."

"Yes, well perhaps I just thought it sounded good. But I cannot subscribe to the belief that I was somehow responsible for recruiting him. It was, if I recall, Rex's idea, although I admit that he happened to fill a need."

"He fitted perfectly."

"You have a very easily-satisfied level of perfection, Alec," said Q, slumping into his chair. "Let us just say he fitted. At the time. That does not remove the fact that I have always felt uneasy about him and that I continue to do so. He is not a man of calibre."

"But you didn't want a man of calibre. You wanted a lazy man, an indolent idiot who's happy to get his pay, do the minimum required and who wouldn't think of asking questions, least of all intelligent ones. The last thing you want is a chap with ambitions."

"Well there's certainly little chance of our George having any of those. If he ever had any ambition it got drained out of him at the time we found him. His amazing ability to cock up a business in so comprehensive a way must surely have become apparent, even to him."

"It was rather spectacular, wasn't it?" Tenison laughed his snorting giggle. "Difficult to see how he could have lost money faster than he did."

"Typical of his type. How like a social climber with, frankly, the background and breeding of an oik, to have the pretentious idea of being a wine-shipper. Only someone of his sort would try to flog the stuff to the Muslims. A child of seven could have seen that he hadn't a hope, but not George. What's more, he couldn't even see what to do when it dawned on him that the stuff wasn't selling. Far from cutting his losses, he buys higher-quality hooch because he thinks that the Arabs will go for that. This is the man whom we recruit to work our Middle East run."

"Who doesn't even know he's been recruited."

"Who has not the slightest idea what he's doing. Who thinks his business has been taken over in some way that guarantees his job and his salary but who has still not thought to ask why he has to meet supposed wine-buyers in hotel bars, not to discuss the vendange but to hand over the packets which arrive with his bottles and who, more to the point, has managed to persuade himself that wine-drinkers, with millions of bottles of French wine available just across the Channel, are somehow going to develop a taste for wines from where? From the Lebanon? Where next? The outback? This man is too bad to grace the name of failure."

Q smirked to himself. That had sounded quite good.

"Since we have nothing from the wire-service," he went on, "I suppose we must assume that the good George has finally failed us."

"Do try to keep that note of triumph out of your voice."

"I assure you that it gives me no satisfaction whatsoever. It means more work for us. We shall now have to decide what we are to do about this situation. And, since I cannot think that George any longer fills any useful function perhaps the time has come for his position to be terminated."

Tenison looked at Q quickly. "And George?" he asked. "What about George?"

"Indeed," murmured Q. "And George."

TWO

AUGUST 12, WEDNESDAY
BEIRUT

George and Tom were both unusual in that neither shared
the standard colonial taste for gin and tonic or whisky and
soda. They both much preferred wine. This was
particularly singular since most wine imported in England
was ludicrously expensive claret or burgundy and the
recent burst of interest in cheaper wines had led to a
superfluity of vile blends which European vignerons were
happy to offload onto willing and wide-eyed wine-buyers.
Wine, in England, was a joke. Q had been deliberately
wrong in some of the things he had said to Tenison; where
he was unwittingly wrong was on the wine-producing
potential of the Lebanon. As it happened it had a fine soil
and, more important, an ideal climate for the production of
good grapes with excellent acidity. The long warm
summers and plentiful spring rain made for grapes of great
succulence, notably cabernet sauvignon, merlot and
cinsault in which the late summer sun developed the
sugars. Some local farmers even claimed that the
chardonnay so central to the burgundy was an offshoot of
the luscious obaideh grape, now well-known thanks to the
success of Château Musar. Even in the first growths of
Bordeaux some winemakers were known surreptitiously to
add sugar to the vats for chaptalisation; in Lebanon there
was no need. Wines were not produced in great quantity
but there was enough to satisfy a small and appreciative

market in the Middle East.

George had come to Beirut in 1950, thanks to a lucky posting at the end of his National Service. Gazetted into the RASC, he had spent eighteen wretched months in Catterick at the bleak end of Yorkshire, learning to drive and, having learned, ferrying 3-tonners full of supplies from depots to NAAFIs and barracks. Apart from earning him his HGV licence, which had been of no further use to him, the job had also introduced him to basic supply-accounting and stock-taking. So it was that when, just as he was resigned to seeing out his service in the chill rigours of Bapaume Barracks, a corporal-clerk in the Beirut NAAFI was discovered to have been running a small but enjoyable scheme which involved selling bottles of IPA to a local brothel, George's platoon sergeant had suggested him as a replacement on temporary duty.

George, with no family and no particular friends, had been pleased to go and delighted with what he found. Anywhere would probably have seemed an improvement on Catterick but the warmth and the easy indolence of life in the Middle East appealed instantly and enduringly. After demob, which he had managed to delay for three months to make the most of the Army's not-ungenerous overseas allowances, he arranged to stay on in Beirut where, thanks to his NAAFI contacts, he found a job as a stores-clerk with a small supermarket, one of the first to open in competition with the traditional markets. Rather to his surprise, trade was good and George took on responsibility for buying various lines, including drink, and for managing the second and third stores which opened over the next seven or eight years. It was then that his characteristic lack of ambition deserted him. Normally happy to let life take its course and to deal with events as they happened, he decided unwontedly to determine his own future. He had seen the rise in sales of drink at the supermarket, had noticed the steady increase in the number of Europeans who bought there as the Lebanese wine-growers developed in confidence and skill, and thought that the time was ripe to go into the wine business himself. Since his first job after school had been in a brewery he was confident at least in his knowledge of beer. Could the principles of wine-selling be so very different? Raising a small loan from a local bank, he set up a company to buy the wine direct from the producers, many of whom he had come to know over the years, to sell it direct to the Europeans and, more important, export it to Europe.

He made a number of mistakes. His market research consisted entirely of his own hunches; he had no real idea of the state of the market for Lebanese wines in Europe. He simply thought that people ought to like it. He had expected his contacts in the trade to let him have good stuff; they did not, preferring to keep that for their existing customers. Instead they invited him to sample what they called everyday wines, which they assured him would be much to the taste of his customers at home. Finally, since the supermarkets began to buy in bulk, he could not hope to match their prices and he rapidly began to lose money. Q had been nearly right about George's next move, although it was not quite as he said. All that had happened was that, perhaps knowing that it was too late, the producers had suddenly agreed to let him have their better quality bottles. But he had showed three months of steady losses and the bank had already warned that, in another month, it would pull the plug.

Throughout the entire business, for all his self-confessed pessimism, George had tenaciously believed that there was a market for the wine, a belief almost entirely based on his own developing taste for the stuff. At home he had drunk beer because everyone did and, in Beirut, had done so because it had not occurred to him to drink anything else. But the producers had in time won him over and, to his own surprise, he had come to love the buttery whites and the silky reds which had seemed so much to sum up the heavenly country which was now his home. His principle was that, if an ordinary uneducated bloke like him liked these wines, then so would an awful lot of others.

Now he and Tom sprawled in deck chairs on the brown lawn high in the hills above the Bekaa valley outside the Ksara Hotel. They swigged with deep pleasure at a young chardonnay, one of several they had tried this evening.

"Fancy a case or two of this? asked Tom.

"Too damn right, guvnor." George replied, "Magnificent, isn't it? I really think we could shift a few of these."

"Business doing well these days?"

"Very fair, thanks. Can't complain."

It was true that, some years ago now, business had quite suddenly taken a puzzling turn for the better. As he was bracing himself for the reality of bankruptcy, and wondering what its consequences would be, he had had a phone call from the British Embassy. The man did not identify himself beyond saying that he had been talking to Mr Jacobson, the commercial attaché, and had been led to believe that Mr Spofforth had a rather interesting line in local wines. George had agreed, adding that the prices at the moment were alarmingly good. The man said that he would like to place an order for some. When George asked him when he would like to come down for a tasting, he said that he didn't really have time for that; perhaps

George would be so good as to use his discretion to make up a mixed case or two.

"It's for one of the commercial attaché's business contacts," he had gone on. "I gather he isn't particularly choosy but he remembers drinking some Lebanese wine on holiday and rather liking it."

"Fair enough." George had said, "Leave it to me. Two cases was it?"

"I think we'd better make it ten."

"Ten? He's got a good thirst, your friend, if you don't mind my saying so."

"Yes. No, he, er, runs a restaurant. In Hampshire. And will probably wish to place further orders if he's happy with what you supply."

"No problem at all," said George, grinning to himself. "Would you like a quote for all that?"

"No, the price is not a problem. If you would just send the invoice to Mr Jacobson at the embassy."

George had had no dealings before with the embassy but, in so far as he'd ever thought about the people within it, he had imagined that they might sound like this chap. Nasal, austere, lofty and about as warm as a snowman's armpit. He had come across their sort in the Army. Some made good officers but most had been genetically incapable of unbending sufficiently to breathe the air at NCO level or below. George had made up the ten cases and dispatched them to the embassy. To his pleasure and surprise, two weeks later he had received an embassy cheque which had gone some way to keeping Salim at the bank at bay.

Three weeks after that he had had another call from the nasal anonymous. Mr Jacobson's contact had very much enjoyed the wine, he said, and would like Mr Spofforth to be his regular supplier. Would he be prepared to take this on? Christ, George had said, pardon my French, he got through that lot fast didn't he? Hundred and twenty bottles in just over a month? What's he doing, filling his swimming pool?

"He's only drunk a couple of bottles," said the nose, "but he was delighted with them. They brought back happy memories."

"Righto," said George, "how many cases would he like?"

"What do you think?" the voice replied. "How many cases do you sell in an average month?"

"Cases? Not that many. Turnover in a good month is about a couple of hundred bottles, say fifteen or sixteen cases."

"Therefore, if we, Mr Jacobson's contact, were to order say fifteen cases a month, you could supply them?"

"No problem."

"And that would, how shall I put it, help your cash flow?"

"Of course. If I can be frank, it would make the whole business a whole lot easier. But, if I may ask, is this about getting a good deal for your friend or doing me a favour?"

"The role of the British Embassy, as I'm sure you're aware, is to spread the word about the values of the British way of life. It is also to make certain that we protect the interests of our citizens."

"Well, no complaints about that."

"Good. Would you arrange to have them shipped direct to Southampton from now on? Repeat orders will be given to you by one of my colleagues. One or two of our embassy staff may also wish to come down to your store from time to time for a tasting. Would that be all right?"

"No problem."

"Good. Jolly good." The voice sounded almost friendly. "Oh, by the way, do you ever read the English papers?"

"Every now and then. I sometimes pop up to the consulate library and read them there. Of course they're usually a day late by the time they get there."

"Yes, it's inconvenient, isn't it? Well, look. From time to time we make contact with our embassy staff through the personal column of the Times."

"What, births marriages and deaths?"

"Not quite." The chill returned. "We find the personal column a very useful way of keeping in touch with our staff, some of whom are often on the move, upcountry or abroad and out of telephone contact."

"I see. Clever idea."

"We find it works. So long as they can get hold of a copy of the paper, which fortunately is available more or less throughout the Middle East, even if we don't know precisely where they are, we can get a message to them."

"And this affects me in some way, does it?"

"It does. We may, from time to time, ask you to meet a member of the embassy staff and so might use the personal column to contact you. Your contact in London uses the code-name Q."

"Very mysterious. Why not just write to me?"

"Because our man, or woman, has to see the ad too so that they know where to go and when."

"Why not send them here?"

"That may not always be convenient." The chill deepened. "I think you understand, Mr Spofforth that this is a very important order to you and that our business methods must be a matter for us to determine. I believe you might decide that it was wiser to accept our way of doing business without asking too many questions."

"Fine by me. Your problem, not mine."

"A very healthy attitude. Every now and then someone from the embassy may bring you a small package. Or it may be sent to you. Perhaps you would be so kind to pass these on as instructed."

"No point in asking what the packages are, I take it?"

"As you say. None whatever. Oh, incidentally, you might like to know that, as a supplier to the embassy, you will be an ex officio member of the diplomatic staff. As such you will be afforded the embassy's protection should the need ever arise."

"Blimey. Why should it arise, if you don't mind my asking?"

"I'm sure it won't, Mr Spofforth. But this is the Middle East where life, as I'm sure you have found, is never quite as stable or predictable as at home. There are always a few unhappy people who wish her majesty's government ill. Always best to be prepared. Apropos of which, I will arrange for you to have a copy of a little book which we have prepared for embassy staff. It has some helpful information on the procedures to follow should you ever run into any kind of difficulty."

"What kind of info?"

"Oh, you know, numbers to ring, places to go, codes, that

sort of thing."

"Codes? All a bit James Bond isn't it?"

"Don't let your imagination run away with you, Mr Spofforth. It's all very hypothetical. Goodbye. We'll be in touch."

George was intrigued but not puzzled by the conversation. He knew enough about the world to know that business transactions were seldom straightforward or even comprehensible to those outside their remit. He was essentially honest and had never felt the need to fiddle or pilfer from any employer. At the same time he knew that others ran their lives in different ways and, so long as he wasn't involved in actual crime, understood that rules could be flexible. If, as it seemed in this case, it was the embassy who was doing the bending, well what was he to do but go along with it as a loyal British citizen? The nasal voice might not have much by way of personality but he did have a certain style, something that seemed to be sadly lacking in the UK as he understood it these days.

Suez had been the turning point he thought. He had watched, on the small television in the back room at the supermarket, the hazy telefilm of British soldiers storming the beaches near Port Said and the French bombers overhead. It had seemed ludicrous and vainglorious, less a conviction invasion than an attempt to recapture the style and panache of D-Day and Anzio, to make the nation feel good about itself. Its, to him, inevitable failure only served to remind the world that Britain was an old dog, too old to learn new tricks and remorselessly playing the old ones over and over again despite its failing eyesight and toothless drooling jaws. Britain was done for, George realised, and nothing would ever be the same again.

It was summed up perfectly by the motor industry. In George's youth Britain's economy was built in part on the back of the elite team of motor-manufacturers, run by imaginative and enlightened men who knew the market, cared unsentimentally for the workforce, and produced cars which the public wanted to buy. Then some money-man, ignorant of the motivational power of working for an identifiable team, decided that they would work better if they merged. As the mergers increased so the identities weakened and the workers lost the pride in what they were doing. Quality, reliability and demand fell. Now the cars looked the same and were noteworthy only for their unreliability. Morris, Austin, Wolseley, Riley, Rover, Triumph, Hillman were now no more than cyphers, the bulk product of something called British Leyland. What was wonderful was that they'd had designed, probably at huge cost, a new trademark. They had not however realised that the designer, no doubt an embittered subversive, had presented them with nothing less than an elegant plughole. It was a perfect and poignant symbol of how Britain was going down the drain.

It annoyed him that a country could have such pretensions and get things so wrong. At least out here you knew it wasn't going to work. In England you were teased into thinking it might just. He had reached the point some time ago where he realised, with no feeling of shame or surprise, that he didn't want to be associated with England any more. He missed the place he used to know but it was a country he didn't want to go back to.

He thought derisively of the curious coves who were running it. He remembered being mildly excited once by the talk about one nation. In a funny way, that old Edwardian throwback Macmillan had understood the problems. He was in the mould of those nobby officers who nonetheless understood their men and won their confidence and respect. In his lofty way he had managed to see the inequalities and, from his patrician perch, had tried to balance things up. But he'd gone and a new kind of politician was arriving, people more interested in their own careers than in old-fashioned notions like public service; cynical second-raters who didn't even bother to pretend that they were interested in the people or what they thought. They didn't even pay us, he thought, the courtesy of minding whether we believed what they told us.

George glanced at Tom who was gazing quietly out into the distance. Here was a man in whose simple humanity was ingrained an unquestioning sense of his good fortune at having been born British. In his blood pulsed the corpuscles of nationhood. George thought of him as the notional Britisher, representative of all the things Britain thought it stood for: stiff upper lip, common sense, humanitarian values, never kick dogs, treat the wogs firm but fair, standing up for the national anthem, the notional anthem.

Out here at least he wasn't implicated. England could do what it liked and, because he wasn't there to vote the buggers in, he could not be tarnished, it was nothing to do with him. And the Lebanese? He thought, are they cocking up their own country? Not my problem, old son; it's their country and they can do what they like to it. I want to be innocent and uninvolved. I'm the archetypal innocent abroad.

A few days after his conversation with the man from the embassy, a small parcel had been delivered to his office. Inside was a small book with a plain blue cover which bore the words, Notes for Diplomatic Staff. George found that it was rather more Fleming-like than his contact had led him to believe. The introduction sought to reassure its readers that everything that followed was, like World War III, extremely unlikely to happen but, in the remote possibility that it did, here were some helpful guidelines. Numbers to call if you felt you were the subject of unwelcome attention from the locals; destinations to aim for if a swift exit seemed appropriate, codes for discreetly British-owned buildings. George was quietly pleased that the Times classified also got a mention. It was actually quite a good read – certainly better than the War Office directives he had been used to in the Army. Perhaps it was his military training but, for whatever reason, he had thought it only courteous to memorise some of the procedures.

Tom snorted suddenly as he struggled with wakefulness and looked at his watch.

"Good Lord, is that the time?" he muttered apologetically from force of habit.

Oh, bugger. "What is the time, old boy?"

"Coming up for three."

"Just remembered I need to make a call. Had a bit of trouble with a couple of Arabs who liked the look of my package and tried to help themselves."

"Good God, is that normal?"

"It happens. It used to worry me but I suppose it's par for the course. If you're on the edge the chances are you're close to someone else's pitch. Anyway nothing serious so far. Just need to alert a couple of people. Shan't be a tick. Why don't you get another bottle while I'm away?"

George walked to the bar.

"Fii talafoon?" he asked.

"Fii." The barman nodded. He reached down and put an old bakelite instrument on the counter.

"Shukran," said George. He lifted the receiver and waited.

"Ah, yes," he said at length "Bayruut waahid, thamaanya, ithneen thalaatha, sitta, sitta."

He waited, winking reassuringly at Tom.

"Hello? Ahmed? It's George. Can you hear me? Right."

AUGUST 13, THURSDAY
LONDON

Q pressed a button on the squawkbox on his desk.

"Angela, would you ask Mr Tenison to come up right away please?"

"He's already on his way up." came his secretary's voice from the desk.

"Is he? Good. Have we heard from George, do you know?"

"I gather we have. That's why Mr Tenison is coming up. In fact he's just walked in. Shall I..?"

"Send him in, would you?"

Tenison came in. He had a sheet of paper in his hand.

"Morning, Q."

"What does he say?" asked Q.

"Nothing very constructive, I'm afraid." He put the paper on the desk in front of Q who read it swiftly.

August 10 meeting failure due limpet. Refix alternative contact/location. George.

"What bloody limpet?" asked Q.

"I asked myself the same question."

"What does he know about limpets? Who's been talking to him?"

"I thought it wise to check with our people in Beirut just now," said Tenison carefully. "I gather there's a semi-official manual they hand out to their people. It has basic instructions on survival and a few simple codes. They thought it probable that George had been given one. There's no absolute certainty, of course."

"There's pretty little certainty about very much, Alec. In fact there's rather an embarrassing number of questions to answer, not least, if George really has attracted someone's attention, which if you recall was most of the point of his being there at all, what are we doing to find out who it is who's interested and what their current moves are?"

"As you may recall, Q, there was a contingency plan for just this… contingency."

"I'm aware of that, Alec. I drew it up. What I'm asking is whether anyone has done anything to check whether it needs to be put into action."

"I'll make some calls at once."

"Please. The first thing is that we can't keep the girl hanging around, especially if someone is following George. She may have been seen and, if she is seen again, someone may put two and two together. But we need to know precisely what is going on in Beirut. The plan was to call Peter in at this stage and that's what we shall do."

"Do we know where he is?" asked Tenison.

"Not exactly. But the Middle East is his patch so he ought to be able to get to Beirut from wherever he is within two or three days."

"Won't that be a bit late? Especially if someone is watching George."

"Can't be helped," said Q with a tiny shrug. "We can't assume that Peter is within easy range. If he's in Lebanon or Israel then clearly there isn't a problem, but if he's playing the girls in Persia again, he'll need all the time he can get."

"Fair enough," said Tenison. "In any case I suppose we shouldn't necessarily conclude that George has lost control. It's always possible that he has spotted something suspicious and is lying low until he hears from us."

"Alec, you're such a gentleman," said Q, his voice silky with irony. "So trusting and ready to see the good in people, particularly where it patently doesn't exist. For myself, I shall be happy if George manages to understand the message and hasn't lost his recognition key."

"And let's hope that Peter is keeping his eyes on the paper."

"Thank you, Alec," said Q without a smile. "I'll call you when I hear anything."

AUGUST 14, FRIDAY
TRIESTE

> George in Beirut. Le Vendome Hotel bar 17 August 11pm. Peter in horn-rims. Recognition seven. Q.

Sunshine poured through the open porthole of the yacht. A shaft of it fell bleaching the shoulders of the blond man in his early thirties who lay sprawled on the double bunk. He rolled onto his back and squinted at the Rolex on his wrist. He raised an elbow and gently nudged the sleeping girl beside him. She groaned and opened an eye.

"Hello," she said.

The man nudged her more firmly. "It's after half-past twelve, sweetie. Go and get the papers, hey? I'll make the breakfast."

The girl groaned again but climbed out of bed, pulled a shirt over her head and, shuffling on a pair of flip-flops, climbed the stairs out of the cabin. He followed her closely and, standing amidships in the little galley, watched her appreciatively as she walked yawning across the boardwalk of the Marina Cavour, past the serried lines of yachts drawn up as if for official review, and across the small piazza to the single all-purpose shop. He whistled cheerfully and began to make coffee. It was a beautiful day and she was a very pretty girl.

After a few minutes she emerged from the shop and walked slowly back to the yacht. Her short dark hair was fluffed by the light morning breeze as she walked, reading La Stampa, another newspaper tucked under her arm. She smiled at the man as she climbed aboard and they cuddled warmly.

"Thank you, cara mia," he said as she gave him his paper. It was yesterday's Times.

"Niente, carissimo."

She sat on deck and read her paper. The man glanced at the front page of the Times while the espresso spurtled on the stove. Almost as an afterthought, as he rose to collect the pot, he flipped the paper over and began to skim through the small ads.

"Senti, Peter!" the girl exclaimed excitedly. "Lucio Dalla canta a Trieste! Next week! Shall we go, darling?" She came to stand beside where he sat.

"I'd love to, sweetie," said Peter, "but I don't know if I shall be here. I've just discovered that I'm double booked. I have to visit relatives in the Lebanon." He stroked her bottom almost absent-mindedly. "Ah well, arrivederci, Trieste. I wonder what the hell recognition seven is."

AUGUST 14, FRIDAY
BEIRUT

It was just after nine in the evening and, although the sun had mercifully dipped some hours ago behind the houses, still hot. George enjoyed the heat and, as he walked slowly along the narrow street which led to the Hotel Commodore, the apartment block where he lived, he smiled to himself. It was not an imposing hotel like the Beau Rivage but it had nonetheless the pretensions of a small porch and a bleak reception area, not unlike the small hotels you find in most English cities. As George made his slightly wobbly way across the hall he did not notice the small man sitting on a hard chair pretending to read Al Ahram. George went to the desk and smiled thinly at the porter who greeted him with unaccustomed warmth.

"Ah, Mr Spofforth! Good evening, sir!"

"Hello, Mehdi. Any messages?"

"Messages? Ah yes, let me see. Number 213, isn't it? Number 213."

"As ever is," said George, faintly puzzled.

The porter fumbled among the pigeon-holes behind him. As he did so George turned back and stared across the lobby. He saw the Arab who had put down his paper and was looking in his direction. As he caught George's eye he quickly picked up his paper again. George squinted at him, trying to place him. Light dawned as he turned back to the desk.

"Thank you, Mehdi," he said heavily. "Very thoughtful."

He moved away from the desk and started towards the lift. The Arab stood up and began to move towards George. George, however, abruptly changed direction and turned through a door off the lobby. It was the gents. He locked himself into a cubicle and sat down, breathing heavily, just as the Arab came in from the lobby. George put his head in his hands.

"Oh, damn and blast," he said under his breath.

There was no sound from outside the cubicle. George sighed and read some Arabic graffiti on the wall.

"Dirty little sod," he muttered.

After a few moments he cautiously got up and tried to look through a crack in the cubicle door. Unfortunately the configuration of the crack offered him only a view straight ahead of the yellowing porcelain of the urinal. It was impossible to squint to the left towards his follower. He climbed gingerly onto the bowl hoping to see over the top but the cubicle was too long to allow him to see more than the top of the partition and he sat down again wearily. After another two minutes or so, during which he heard no sound from beyond the cubicle, he stood again and began very gently to ease back the bolt. It squeaked suddenly and he froze. After a pause he tried again; again it squeaked, again he froze. At the third attempt he managed to slide the bolt all the way back and, leaning his shoulder against the door in case the man tried to charge him, he very gradually opened the door a tiny crack and looked through. The Arab was leaning against the washbasin, his arms folded, watching George's door intently. He seemed quite relaxed as if time was not a problem for him. He didn't move, although he had certainly seen George's door open. George slid the bolt back rapidly and sat down again. This was absurd. On the other hand he was in no hurry either. Time was, in the end, probably on his side. Nonetheless he was both bored and angry. It was a stupid way to spend an evening. He got out his wallet and leafed through the assortment of papers within it; there was nothing worth reading which would divert him for more than a minute. He tidied his banknotes and was putting them back in order when he heard the cloakroom door open and someone come in. He jumped up and quietly opened the cubicle door a crack. He saw to his delight that it was another of the porters with whom he was on good terms. The Arab had turned round and was washing his hands in the basin. George shouted through the crack.

"Abdul, dear old fruit! It's me, Mr Spofforth. Will you do me a favour and deal with this chap for me? He wants me to go to bed with him. I've told him I'm not that sort of fellow but he won't go away."

The porter turned without a word to the Arab and slapped him hard across the face, shouting angrily at him and pushing him against the wall.

"So sorry, Mr Spofforth," he broke off to say. "I send this bad man away."

George emerged rapidly from his cell and walked fast to the door as the two men grappled.

"Good lad, Abdul," he said. "Well done. I think you might have a word with Mehdi. I think he may have put this chap up to this. Must rush. Thanks again."

He pushed through the lobby and outside. He walked quickly down the street and turned the corner towards the harbour. (Andrew wasn't sure what the harbour in Beirut looked like but imagined it as a warmer version of the Liverpool docks.) George looked back and saw the Arab coming fast out of the hotel and heading in his direction.

"Oh, hell's teeth," muttered George and broke into the

closest he could come to a run. It was not at all bad for someone as stocky as him but the Arab was a little younger and much fitter. Under the convention that films conveniently use to shorten the distance between major landmarks, George reached the docks in a matter of moments. He ducked round the corner of a warehouse and into an alcove. There was barely any light, just a slight spill from the few lamps. After a moment the Arab pounded past. George counted three and then puffed as quietly as he could back the way he had come. The Arab meanwhile had reached the second corner of the warehouse and checked, looking out over the black water. He began to lope cautiously along the waterside lee of the building. George continued in the other direction and, as he reached the waterside, he waited, trying to flatten his heaving bulk against the wall. There were no further obliging alcoves. The Arab reached the end of the waterside wall and paused again looking around him and back over the water. As he did so George, playing cleverly to his strengths, ran at him and barged him bodily into the water. There was a shout and a splash, then more shouting. George peered down into the darkness.

"It's your own fault the water tastes so bloody foul," he shouted. "You shouldn't run your sewage straight into the sea. Filthy habit."

He limped away, his ballooning shirt sticking wetly to his back.

Later, back in his room, having sought out Abdul and pressed two hundred lire into his hand, George packed hurriedly. His pockets bulged with odd bits of paper. He crammed a small blue book into his jacket pocket, sat on the lid of his suitcase and looked rather wildly round the room.

"That'll have to do, old boy," he said to himself. "Come on."

He shut his door and hurried down the corridor. He stopped at the lift for a moment.

"In times of emergency, never use the lift," he muttered. "Remember the drill. You ought to know that by now, old boy."

He puffed to the stairs and started down. As he did so the lift doors opened and the man who had followed him the other day emerged. He walked purposefully down the corridor looking at the room numbers. George lumbered the rest of the way down the stairs, back through the lobby and yet once more out into the street. Even the area round the Commodore was busy, although it was not close to the areas the tourists liked to see. But it had its own relaxed culture, its own commerce of girls and music and drugs, a community of pleasure and relaxation and, because it was tourist-free, had none of the supercilious servility of the city-centre. They were their own people here. The streets were full of happily ambling Lebanese, taking the air in an elegant Levantine passeggiata. There was no call for taxis here but, because he is pretty much the hero of the story, George was lucky. A taxi passed. It was empty. George flagged it down and climbed in.

THREE

AUGUST 17, MONDAY
BEIRUT
THE VENDÔME HOTEL

It is a curious fact that the bars of smart international
hotels in warm countries seem to invite those who drink in
them to adopt a sort of post-colonial safari uniform.
Middle-aged men whose closest encounter with the bush
might be the passenger seat of a Land Rover, sported khaki
drill and, if they were there long enough, grew moustaches
and affected a sort of military drawl in their speech. It was
precisely at them that the Range Rover would one day
soon be so accurately targeted, poignantly the last smart
move of the car industry which George so scorned.

Among the would-be game hunters lounging by the bar of
the Vendôme tonight stood a tall broad-shouldered man.
We last saw him naked aboard a boat off Trieste but this
evening he was distinctive by the lightweight suit he wore
in preference to safari gear. He ran his fingers through his
short fair hair and adjusted the horn-rimmed glasses he
wore as he read his folded copy of the Times. He glanced
at his watch – it was twenty-five past eleven – and drained
the glass of beer in front of him. He called the barman
over.

"My name's Van Straten." He sounded South African. "I'd
arranged to meet some friends here, a Mr Wilkinson and a
lady. Has anybody left a message for me?"

"No, sir," said the barman. "No messages. No visitors. Sorry."

Peter left the hotel and took a taxi to the Commodore. He leaned back in his seat and consulted a small blue book which had the look of an extended index. At the hotel he went up to the desk.

"Evening," he said. "I'm due to meet Mr Spofforth. Which room is he?"

"213, sir. Second floor."

Peter ran up the stairs. He found 213 and tapped a code on the door. Silence. He tried again; still nothing. Pulling out a set of skeletons he opened the door and slipped cautiously inside. Devastation. The cramped little suite, in truth no more than a small bedroom cum office, had been clumsily ransacked, probably without success since there seemed to be little in the way of papers or clothing to scatter. The desk cupboard was empty and Peter wrenched at the half-open wardrobe door. Inside on a hanger swung a single red dress.

Peter picked up the phone.

"Reception. This is room 213. I'd like an international call, please. The Times of London."

That evening, alone in the flat, Andrew turned again to the typewriter and leafed through the cuttings from the Times. In his mind's eye he could see the double arc of the glass roof over Lime Street station and the counterpoint of passengers weaving across the bleak concourse.

AUGUST 18, TUESDAY
HAYDARPASA STATION, ISTANBUL

It was surprisingly cool in the glorious spaciousness of the station, half Teutonic castle half temple. Andrew had been back to the library to look at their atlases. From what he could tell it would be possible for George, assuming he was lucky, and Andrew would take care of that, to get a ferry from Tripoli, fifty miles up the road to the Turkish port of Mersin and thence by train and bus to Istanbul in around twenty-four hours. It was thus now around eight in the evening in Istanbul. A train pulled in. Passengers stumbled off, stretching, many in burnouses but a good number wearing European-style suits and jackets. As such the rotund figure of the essentially English George, sweating, dishevelled and carrying a brown suitcase aroused no attention.

Somewhere in George's memory was the idea that, in an emergency, the best course of action was to travel fast and far. In his fuzzy way he realised that taking a plane was not an option; the journey to the airport and the inevitable hanging around the concourse would have left him savagely exposed. A ferry seemed a less obvious means of escape and Istanbul would be somewhere he could lose himself. He had thus spent a sweaty hour in a taxi to Tripoli. Six hours on the ferry had enabled him to catch his breath and think what to do. Now, hot and tired but somehow in control, he walked towards a newspaper stand.

"Times please," he said.

The man stared at him and shrugged.

"Times of London?" George tried.

The man shrugged again and pointed at a rack where a number of battered American and European papers were displayed. George riffled through them, found a copy of the day before's edition and glanced rapidly at the front page. After a moment he put it back, smiled cheerily at the shopkeeper and walked away. Leaving the station he walked heavily down to the ferry terminal and, in due course, steamed across the Bosphorus to Kabatas and the short walk to the grey Soviet-style bulk of the Istanbul Hilton.

Inside the lobby he asked the receptionist for the phones; she smiled and pointed to a cabin in the corner of the lobby. George went in and dialled a number.

"Hello? Times? Classified please."

> Q. George missing. Commodore room ransacked –
> radio gone. Le Vendome contact 17 August failed.
> Instructions? Peter.

Q was, at roughly the same moment, reading the Times which was spread out in front of him on the desk. Someone had ringed the relevant ad in felt tip.

"The question is, Alec, where's the man likely to go?"

"With respect, sir," said Tenison, "isn't it more important to know what happened in Beirut?"

"Absolutely right. But until we get hold of George it's going to be anybody's guess as to what did happen. By the way, how did he come to have a radio?"

"He didn't as far as I know. Peter must be guessing."

"Did we ever give George any proper training?"

"Training? No. He had a standard induction and, if you recall, the embassy gave him the basic code book. But, if you recall, the idea was that he shouldn't have any clear idea of how he was being used. I'm not certain that he was ever told what the codebook was."

"Pity. If he had been trained we might have some inkling as to how he'd behave."

"I should have thought the only predictable thing about George was that he will do the unpredictable." Tenison smirked.

George was, as it happened, in his room sampling a bottle of dry resinated Turkish wine.

Q. Enforced departure Beirut. Arrived Istanbul, staying Hilton using passport five. New contact/ location urgent. George.

The next morning Q enjoyed Tenison's reaction to George's ad.

"I hope you're impressed," Q said. "Not a bad move at all. Good place to go to ground, Istanbul. And passport five, clever stuff. I'm impressed he remembered to change his identity."

"It's all in the book," said Tenison dismissively. "And the

only problem is that everyone else will know he's changed it. More particularly where he is now."

"Yes, well quite. The important thing is to fix him up with a cover. Who's nearest?"

"We don't have anyone in Turkey at all. Vesna was the one he was meant to rv with at the Beau Rivage last week. A bit dangerous to expose her again. There's Leila but she's in Hungary. It would take time to contact her and then she's got to get to Turkey."

"How long, do you think?"

"With luck we might reach her this evening on the six o'clock sweep. She could be in Istanbul by next Monday."

"All right, I'll go for that. Will you contact George by the earliest possible classified? They can meet in Izmir. Find a good rv will you?"

AUGUST 21 FRIDAY

> George in Istanbul. Buyuk Efes Hotel, Izmir. 24 August, 6pm. Female contact, cigarette holder. Recognition two. Q.

In the air-conditioned vacuousness of the bar at the Istanbul Hilton George finished his glass and scowled at the Times he'd had sent over.

"What a load of bollocks," he muttered to himself. "Izmir I ask you. I've only just got here." He waved at the barman.

"How far is it from here to Izmir, old fruit?"

"To Izmir, sir? Not so far. About six hundred kilometre. But is not good road for car."

"No problem, old cock. I'm going by train. There are trains I take it?"

"Oh yes, sir. At least three every day. You take ferry to Bandirma then train; maybe eight hours."

"Do you know a hotel there called the Buyuk Efes?"

"Oh yes, sir. Very smart hotel. Good view of sea. Plenty Americans."

"Americans, eh?" He turned to the man sitting beside him at the bar. "I met a Yank in a pub in Basingstoke once. He was passing through from Salt Lake City. Christ knows what he was doing in a pub in Basingstoke – or me for that matter – but he turned to me after his third scotch and said "Say bud, do you guys keep Christmas the same day as we do?"

"Keep it?" I said to him. "We were keeping Christmas before you lot were even discovered."

George was not short of conversation, if only of the monologue variety. He was leaning heavily on the bar, holed below the waterline by the excitements in Beirut and the strong Turkish wine. He had regaled the barman with much of his varied repertoire of old jokes. The fact that he had often got the punchlines wrong had not appeared to concern the barman who had long ago perfected the technique of looking interested and alert while his mind was miles away.

George was laughing loudly and swaying dangerously as a

young woman approached the bar. George raised his glass to her in silent approval. She ordered a martini and lit a cigarette while she waited for it. George stared at her, trying to focus his thoughts. He felt that there was something he needed to do. Something to do with the cigarette. Of course, the female contact. But wasn't she meant to have a cigarette holder? He fumbled for his paper but it fell to the floor and he didn't feel strong enough to bend down for it.

"Good evening, my dear," he said as surreptitiously as he could. "Forget the holder did you?"

The girl turned away from him without looking at him.

"No hang on," he said. "It's George. I think we have an appointment."

"Please, if you don't leave me alone I shall call for help."

The barman discreetly dialled a number on the phone beneath the counter.

"No but I am your help," insisted George. "We've got this meeting. At the Buyuk Efes."

"I don't know what you're talking about," said the girl, "we have no meeting and, since you seem a little unclear as to where you are, this is the Hilton not the Buyuk Efes."

She walked away from the bar followed unsteadily by George.

"Isn't it?" he called after her. "You can't rely on anything these days, can you? But, never mind, you're here and I'm here and that's half the battle. Possession is nine-tenths of the ball as my old PT sergeant used to say." Puzzled by her unwillingness to talk to him, he remembered something else.

"Oh God, of course, recognition two." He dug into his inside pocket and began to pull out a small blue book.

Two men had appeared in the bar and began, as discreetly as possible, to hustle George towards the front door.

"Of come on for Christ's sake," George shouted. "Don't let me down. You need to tell me what to do."

A police car drew up outside and a young policeman got out. He shouted at George in Turkish.

"Don't shout, old cock," yelled George, wrestling himself free from his captors who moved off as the policeman approached.

"I can't understand a bloody word you're saying. Shouting only works if you shout at a foreigner. Never the other way round."

"American?" said the policeman.

"Oh, please," said George.

"English? You very drunk. Name?"

"Easy," said George. "Spofforth of that ilk."

"Papers please."

George handed over his passport.

"Your name one more time please."

"Spofforth, old chum."

"Why then you have passport of James Wilkinson?"

"What? Oh, bugger. Look sorry, wrong passport, that's… that's my chum's. Could you hang on a sec? I've got mine upstairs."

"If not your passport, why your picture?" asked the policeman with more aggression than curiosity.

"Um, bit complicated to explain that one. No problem. Um, look…"

"You are staying here? Then we will go upstairs and check what you say."

Another car had drawn up outside. Three men got out, two probably Turks, the third fair-haired and wearing glasses. One Turk went towards the police car while the other two followed George and the policeman into the lift. George looked at them biliously.

"Spot of trouble with the filth I'm afraid," he said apologetically. "No problem. Just left my passport behind. Here we are. My floor I think."

He fumbled for his key. The lift stopped and he and the policeman got out. The other two paused just long enough to switch open the doors before following. As George opened the door to his room the two men drew level, grabbed the policeman from behind, pressing a cloth over his mouth and nose. They pushed George into the room, dragging the policeman behind them.

"Oh bloody hell!" said George in exasperation. "What is it now?"

"Quiet, George. It's all right. Just don't ask questions, hey? Get your kit and let's move. This fellow's pal will be attracting attention any minute now. Doesn't do for a policeman to fall asleep at the wheel."

"Christ, I don't know, what a rum evening," said George rubbing his forehead. "I thought I had a couple of days taking it easy ahead of me. You wouldn't be Peter by any chance?"

"Right first time," said Peter. "Come along. We've got a long day tomorrow."

In the car George fought against sleep. It puzzled him that, after years of meeting female contacts, this was the first time he'd dealt with a man. Peter shed no light on it when George asked him about it.

"No special reason, I think. It's just easier that way. People are still stupid enough not to suspect a pretty girl."

"Suppose so," said George. "We going far?"

"No, no. Just back to my hotel. It's safer there."

"Must say I was glad to see you tonight. Nick of time really. Actually it was the nick of time for you too. Suppose you know I've got to be in Izmir on Monday?"

"Izmir?" said Peter. "Ah no, that plan's been changed. We're staying in Istanbul tonight."

"And then?"

"A little boat-trip. On the Black Sea."

"Good-oh. Suppose we'd better wire in again in the morning."

"Yes, of course. We'll do that."

George felt more himself in the morning. Peter arrived while he was having breakfast.

"Sleep well?" he asked.

"Not bad. At all. What's the plan?"

"We'll go and see about our boat when you're ready."

"I think ought to wire in first, just to let them know the form."

"No need to worry. I've done it already."

George was slightly put out. Wiring in was his thing – and

besides he felt rather pleased with himself for having been responsible enough to remember.

"Pretty smart work," he said. "What did you say?"

"Just a routine code. Said you were safe and asking for instructions. We need to be sure where they want you next. It may be wiser for you to take a bit of a holiday. To let your friends in Beirut settle down a bit."

Even as he spoke, the telex operator, struggling letter by letter through the clearly-written but impenetrable words of Peter's text, slowly and carefully typed onto his machine the message to Q.

August 22

> Q. George now our guest. Will exchange for Alex
>
> within 8 days. Signify agreement. SKVP.

LIVERPOOL

No doubt because they were both nervous, when they met again after her long absence they each drank more than they had meant to.

It was one of those times when it's hard to see the line where affection turns to love. Andrew was aware of how little they knew of each other, that he was gambling on the chance that physical attraction and friendship would mature into something more permanent. They had little enough history but it was all they had in common and, since she had gone abroad so soon after they had met, it was hard for Andrew to decide on the right tone. She was almost a stranger again and yet, if only that one time, they had shared an intense intimacy. He didn't want to know too much about what she'd been doing abroad and was happy to accept her evasive answers, ostensibly not to pry into her privacy but really because he didn't want to uncover other liaisons. So he talked about the party where they'd met, their vaguely mutual friends, in the hope of reviving the original spark. She had cut her hair while she was away, the hair that had first so intrigued him. He murmured how he had loved the weight of it in the shower. She laughed and he was reassured. But she was thinking: "He thinks if he talks about going to bed I'll want to do it again. Nostalgia as aphrodisiac. Nice try, buster."

The restaurant tape was playing popular music from the thirties: You'll Never Know, Me and My Shadow, Some of These Days. So that's what it sounds like, Andrew thought. He remembered reading about it in a Sartre novel years ago and had thought at the time that Sartre had got the title wrong: One of These Days surely? But here it was, something quite different and much much better. Well, well.

They left the Adelphi and walked to his car. He put his arm round her shoulders and, after a moment, she snaked hers round his waist. From the car radio, heavily against the odds but he was due a bit of luck, the unearthly moan of early Miles Davis filtered out like a wisp of cigarette smoke. Outside her flat he leaned across and kissed her. "Any chance of a coffee?" he asked with what he hoped was a joky nonchalance.

"Better not," she said. "Might be better to leave it at this."

"Umm, this being?"

"No complications."

He looked out through the windscreen.

"Sorry to have to press you," he said. "But does this mean that last time was a kind of one-off?"

"Kind of."

"Oh." He waited for her to go on. She didn't.

"Sorry – again – to ask the boring question. Is there, as they say, someone else?"

"That's about it."

"My bad timing again. Well he's a lucky chap."

"Not him, as it happens. Her."

"Ah," he said softly. There was a pause. "Now I can't even feel sorry for myself." If it had another chap it would have been easier. He could have railed against him and felt hard done by and at least it would have felt like an even contest. But this… this wasn't in the rules.

"Do I know her?"

"You might. She's a musician. Plays the violin in the Phil." She turned towards him. "Shall I tell you? Do you mind?"

He made no answer and she went on.

"I was there, quite close to the front and there she was, near the edge of the platform and all I could see was these beautiful biceps. She is pretty and elegant, but it was those lovely arms. I couldn't take my eyes off them."

"Now you know how I feel," he said sombrely.

"Dear Andrew," she said, kissed him quickly and got out of the car.

Some of these days
You'll miss me, honey

AUGUST 24 MONDAY
LONDON

Q's equitable manner had unnervingly given way to something close to indecision. His anger was, without precedent, almost perceptible.

"How the hell did the SKVP of all people get onto this?" It was not, as Tenison knew, a question. Certainly not one which he felt called on or prepared to answer. The frustration that generations of carefully-nurtured administration – he would not insult it by calling it bureaucracy – quite as elaborate and painstaking as anything the Russians could devise, had even now been called into question was something he could appreciate even after only eight years in the service.

Times had changed since Q's early days but Tenison knew enough from the observations of his teachers, lecturers and superiors, of the inexorable process of preparation which, in an ideal candidate, began at the age of eight. The effortless inculcation of the notion of unquestioned superiority of class, nation and race, the development of the unfocussed urge to "do something for the country", to conserve it against any sort of change, the carefully-taught acquisition of acceptable taste, the grounding in classical Latin and Greek with a hint of modern languages, ideally spoken with an accent of such authentic perfection as to soar above accusations that one had gone native. The preservation of some concept of Englishness – Britishness at a pinch – which derived from a view of the world last fashionable around the late 19th century; all this had been Q's study since his childhood and was now at the heart of his approach to life and work. No, not the heart, it was his blood; it pulsed through his arteries and fed his brain. Without it he was nothing.

The effect was to provide an answer to every question, a reaction to every event, a solution to every problem. There was no need to think; it was an automatic process. No need to worry; things would always turn out for the best. And if they didn't then there was always a formula for dealing with that situation. Q and his peers were not so much unflappable as immune from emotion.

And yet and yet… Tenison was conscious, he thought, of an ethereal sine wave of tension in the atmosphere. As though Q knew that, for once and probably never again, he was face to face with a problem for which, if he got it wrong, there was no escape formula. At long last he was being invited to gamble, to risk not just the lives of his juniors but possibly his own as well. And, with a tightening in his balls, Tenison realised that Q was, shockingly, enjoying this unproven experience.

True to the code, none of this was hinted at let alone spoken. Q rubbed a lazy finger across one eyebrow.

"We can't afford, can we, to let them blow George's cover?" he said slowly, reaching inside his jacket for a cigarette case. (Christ what a dinosaur he is, thought Tenison. He's been playing the suave gent so long he actually does it automatically.)

"George is a painfully incompetent, socially undesirable squirt," he said. "Per se. But his importance to us, as an instrument, is paramount. So long as no one knows what he's up to out there he remains invaluable. We therefore have a duty – to ourselves – to protect his position. Do we have a vessel anywhere nearby?"

Tenison lifted a phone.

"No the real question," continued Q as Tenison began to talk quietly into the receiver, "is what to do about Alex. Can we afford to let him go? Don't worry, Alec," he broke off as strangled wavings came from his anguished junior, "that's a rhetorical question. Of course we can't afford to let him go, but do we go through the motions of getting him out, perhaps using Peter, showing them that we're apparently serious, or do we sit tight and risk their thinking that we aren't too concerned about George? It's crucial that they continue to see George as a big fish and deploy the necessary manpower to try to puzzle him out. They must never find out if – when – George becomes dispensable. Any news?"

"There's a 40-foot yacht off Sebastopol now with stores for a month."

"That will do nicely. We'll take the flying boat and join her off Batumi. Will you arrange for Alex to be prepared?"

Tenison paused only fractionally. "When you say we, sir, may I take it that you mean you?"

"Quite right, Alec. Time I took a trip. We shall need to negotiate carefully. You can keep an eye on things here."

Indeed, thought Tenison. After thirty-three years sitting behind a variety of desks it might well be thought time, if not a little overdue, to be leaving the country. The effectiveness of the training was not in dispute; half a lifetime of waiting for the single moment of personal risk and he met it without a whisper.

Q had been writing. Now he handed Tenison a sheet of

standard-issue lined foolscap on which a brief message had been delicately printed in his elegant capitals.

"The Times, dear boy; if you'd be so kind. And would you get me Rex on the phone please."

AUGUST 24, MONDAY
ISTANBUL

George was a happy man. He'd never been to Istanbul, hadn't had the inclination. Turks weren't very much his sort of chaps; that odd mixture of European and Arab, not the sort of fellow a bloke like George could really fathom. It wasn't that he thought they were untrustworthy; he'd lived abroad far too long to have kept that peculiarly English habit of regarding all foreigners as rogues. No, it was just that he couldn't figure out their attitudes, couldn't guess what was going on in their minds. He was happy with your average Arab. They took some knowing; you had to forget everything you'd ever learned about logic and the standard English way of approaching a problem, because the English way wasn't the Arab way. But once you'd learned that the English way wasn't the only way and certainly not always the right way, everything became easier. So he'd come to understand, no, not understand but to appreciate the Arab way of thinking. Different, but no worse than anything he knew.

But, as it turned out, the Turks were a really reasonable bunch. Peter had hardly left his side and, as a newcomer to the city himself, had suggested they spend the day as tourists. George was game enough and they had queued dutifully to see both the Blue and Hagia Sofia mosques. George was amused to see across the way from the latter a crowd of longhaired young men and women outside a ramshackle building calling itself the Pudding Shop. "Heard of that," said Peter. "It's the hippie information exchange. You want to get to Afghanistan or India, that's where you start."

And now, as he sat in the little Physkos bar looking out over the Bosphorus with a glass of raki in front of him, he had few complaints. Peter had explained that it would be best if they both lay low for a few days to let the dust settle in Beirut. It wouldn't matter if the office didn't open for a time; opening hours were famously irregular and a serious buyer would always come back. There seemed to be a chance that they would leave Istanbul in the next day or so and Peter had taken him to see the boat on which they would sail. It looked like the sort of thing George had seen in the harbour in Beirut, the length of an aeroplane with a sheer bow on her like a tea-clipper. She was, he gathered, fully ocean-going but the cruise across the Black Sea was going, in any case, to be a stroll. Not a bad prospect; the trouble with being self-employed was finding the excuse for a holiday so to have one forced on you was very acceptable.

AUGUST 25, TUESDAY

The Times

> SKVP. Agree George/Alex exchange. Will be in yacht off Batumi 31 August. 5am.

The next morning Peter checked them out of the hotel,

took George shopping for replacement clothes and essentials and moved them to the boat.

"I had a message from base," he said. "We have to move to Batumi."

"Know the name," said George. "Just can't place it. Russia I suppose?"

"Close," said Peter. It's right on the Turco-Russian border. Big port. Not a very special sort of place."

"What happens there?"

"We wait a bit more, I'm afraid. Q will be in touch."

"How, as a matter of interest? And how did he reach you here? Through the Times?

"Better than that. I've a short-wave radio on the boat. Part of the basic equipment for this sort of craft. Not very safe way to communicate on land, as you know of course, but, on a boat everyone has radio so it's impossible to trace. We could set off in half an hour or so if you like."

Peter was clearly a practised seaman and George, who knew nothing of boats, was only too happy to sit in the cockpit while Peter nipped from stem to stern, releasing ropes and steering easily away from their mooring and out into the dark green channel of the Bosphorus.

They cruised for over four hours until, at length, the straits (which were in fact the width of a sizeable river) widened swiftly and they pushed out into an expanse of water which stretched from horizon to featureless horizon.

"The Black Sea," said Peter rather unnecessarily as if introducing an old friend.

It was doubly surprising because he had said little throughout the trip and had responded only with short, if not unfriendly, answers to George's questions. This suited George who was much happier having an audience than being one and, since Peter made no interruption, he was able to motor through most of his prejudices and preoccupations in a satisfactorily cathartic way.

It seemed to suit Peter too. Late in the afternoon he slipped the powerful marine engine into neutral and dropped long anchors over the bow and stern.

"This will do for today, I think," he said and went below. Later, after a meal which had reassured George about the quality of boat-food, they sat on the deck drinking coffee.

"I'm afraid I'm not much of a conversationalist," said Peter. "I spend a lot of time on my own, you know, and I seem to have lost the social graces."

"Know how you feel, old son," replied George affably. "I often have days when I can't face talking to people. Anyway, in our business…" he paused conspiratorially," in our business you can't be too careful who you talk to in the first place."

"Dead right," said Peter.

"What's your line. I mean, officially?"

"My line?"

"Yes, I mean I'm a wine merchant as you know. Well always was, long before the boys in London took me on board. But I suppose it's different for you. I'm only a sort of TA, part-time reservist kind of chap, call us up as a last line of defence sort of thing. But I assume you must have some sort of front."

"Oh, yes, I see what you mean. Yes, I charter boats."

"Damn clever. You mean you charter them for other

people or they charter them from you?"

"Both. Whatever seems appropriate."

"That makes sense. So no one knows exactly what you're up to or is at all surprised when you move about."

"Not at all. And, with my radio, I'm in touch as much as I need to be."

"Bloody good. I'm glad some part of the operation seems to work smoothly."

"Doesn't yours?" asked Peter.

"Well, I can't complain seriously I suppose," said George. "After all, once I got out of Beirut it all went pretty well, the rendezvous with you and all that."

"You didn't make it to Izmir, though."

"No but you picked me up even sooner, didn't you? Good thing you were monitoring the messages like a true pro."

"Oh, yes, I keep an eye on the messages."

"Jolly good."

"But you were saying about your end of the operation. Do you find things go wrong?"

"What with?"

"Oh, I don't know. Not so much go wrong as – what? – give the wrong impression. I sometimes feel, I must admit, that London don't really appreciate the problems of the workers on the ground, hey? You know, messages come. Rendezvous change. Be here, collect that, meet this man. I'm pretty sure they think I don't even know I've been recruited. To them I'm just a low-intelligence stooge. Well I know I'm not exactly top-drawer but it doesn't take a genius to put one and one together. Now I'm a solitary sort of fellow, I don't need to be loved and I'm efficient, normally just doing the job is enough. But sometimes I feel I wouldn't mind just a hint of recognition of the fact that we're humans not machines."

"Know exactly what you mean. Cyphers I call us. Rather good I thought, cyphers. We're just numbers to them."

"You right. As I say the job is enough most of the time. But, I wonder, don't you ever get curious?"

"About what?"

"Oh, you know, the bigger picture. What's really going on. Of course we're only a tiny part of a big operation and there's no need for us to know about anything beyond our own unit. It's probably better that way."

"Need to know basis, old son. We're not in the need to know class."

"No, but wouldn't you like to have some ideas about the total game? When you collect your packages and drop them off, do you know why?"

"Not a clue. Gave up wondering a long time ago. Better not to ask. As long as the sales go on, why worry I say."

"Do you even know what's in them?"

"Can't say I do. Used to think it was cash. But I don't think so. Easier to post it. Then I thought it must be drugs and that really gave me the willies. But do you know I somehow don't think it is. You don't know do you?"

"No," said Peter. "Not a clue. But whatever it is there's something really big going on behind it."

"Do you think so?"

"There must be, man. Why else would you have been

followed and nearly kidnapped?"

"Good point. You know I've always thought there was bound to be something a bit shady going on. I mean when was the last time you met someone from the British Embassy you could really trust?"

"My point exactly. So what lies behind it all? Does Q tell you anything?"

"Q? Good Lord no, I've never met him. He just sends the messages. Sometimes. For all I know he may be several different people.

"Do you think so?" asked Peter quickly. "Have you any reason to think that?"

"Not really," said George. "Probably just conspiracy theory. But when you're dealing with a faceless and, as you say, pretty soulless figure whose name is just a letter, it's hard to build up much of a picture of him. In his way he's just a cypher too. And given that he's a cypher I probably wouldn't notice if there were three different chaps all sending messages, all calling themselves Q."

"You don't feel too warm about him then, hey?"

"You could say that. I don't feel anything much most of the time. But if I were less of a natural slob and took offence more easily I might feel rather pissed off by his attitude."

"Why?"

"Hard to pin down. When I left school I worked in a brewery in the East End. We all knew, down with the mash tun or up with the copper, that there was one rule for the management and one for the workers. We got a couple of pints buckshee a day but they never had to buy a pint in their life. We got a rack to park our bikes in and they got a company car. That was the way the world went. And when profits went down if the hop harvest was below par, our pay-rise went down too. Not theirs of course. The management pay-rise never went down because there was always some pressing reason why it shouldn't. Productivity had been good or there was threat of senior staff being poached by a rival brewery or whatever. The net result was that their pay went on going up and ours didn't. Give them bugger all, was their attitude to the workers. Then they can have whatever percentage pay-rise they want. Ten per cent if they like. Because ten per cent of bugger all is bugger all. But that was the way of the world too, we understood that. And we understood it because they always took the trouble to explain to us why they got pay-rises and we didn't. There was always the understanding that we were playing to a set of rules which, to their regret, it was sometimes necessary to adjust. We knew they were cheating and they knew we knew but the game was played and we all knew where we were. Even when they completely ignored a previous undertaking or contradicted something they'd said last week, as long as they took the trouble, not to apologise necessarily, but to go through the motions of a bogus explanation, we accepted it. By and large.

"Now this lot in London, Q and his chaps, don't seem to know that convention. They'll cut your pay, double your workload, ditch long-standing rvs at a day's notice without even bothering to pretend they're sorry or that the rules have been changed. Do you know what I mean? In the old days there was a definite sort of noblesse oblige, they felt they ought to be nice to you even if they didn't need you. This lot can't be buggered to go through the motions of pretending that they care a toss for what you think or feel. The old lot actually wanted you to like them in a funny sort of way. To that extent they really cared. This bunch would be horrified if they thought there was a chance of your liking them. They want you to know the contempt they feel for you. They're in charge, you're shit and that's the way it is. Christ, I didn't much care for paternalism and being patronised rotten but at least you knew they knew you were there. With this lot I don't think they'd notice sometimes, if they trod on us."

He fell silent, then gave a laugh.

"Sorry, old fruit. You rather set me off there. I didn't know I felt so strongly about it."

"Quite understandable, It's easy to get used to being used. Perhaps things will get better."

"Wouldn't bet on it, old son."

"I don't bet. Except on certainties."

Later still, as George sprawled dozing on the deck while the sun set exuberantly over the Istranca Mountains, Peter nudged him gently.

"Time for bed soon, George. We have an early start tomorrow. And we have another rendezvous."

"Not another suit from London I sincerely hope."

"No, a colleague who is also a good friend. I know you'll like her."

George woke the next morning when his head, pressed stiffly against the bulkhead, could no longer tolerate the amplification inside his head of the engine's gentle vibration. He rolled onto his back and gazed at the glowing moiré reflections on the ceiling of the still, ineffable Black Sea.

Peter greeted him with a wave when he went on deck.

"Good morning. I have a principle which is never to wake a sleeping passenger except in an emergency. Just because I love the early morning doesn't mean everyone else has to."

"Can't say I see that many," said George, blinking against the already bright sun. "Not from this angle anyway. I've always thought the only way to see six in the morning is to approach it from midnight and creep up on it. It's much friendlier that way."

Peter laughed and nodded.

"Soon be there now."

Indeed, George could make out that they were heading towards the coast rather than out to sea and he could make out a haze of dancing shapes which were either buildings or spots before his eyes.

"Where's there?" he asked.

"Tsarevo. A medium-sized town, nothing special about it. About twenty miles from the border."

"With? Not much cop at geography."

"Bulgaria."

"Really? Wouldn't mind going there one day. I've heard there are some very reasonable vineyards down in Plovdiv."

"Not so far away." Peter smiled. "But no time to visit this time, you know? Even if they'd let us which is highly doubtful. Bulgaria doesn't offer much of a welcome to non-communists."

"Remind me again what we're doing there."

"Picking up Milena, a very valuable colleague. She's an expert linguist and knows her way round the Balkans better than you know your own face."

"Milena?" Christ, so he hadn't imagined it. Peter really was going to pick up a woman. Oh well, she might be able to cook.

"Yes, she's Yugoslavian, well Slovenian strictly speaking, but she's lived in Italy all her life so that's where she thinks of as home."

"And what exactly is she going to do?" George asked more petulantly than he had intended. He felt vaguely uncomfortable about what he saw as an intrusion.

"I think you'll find she has her uses," said Peter but didn't elaborate.

FOUR

LIVERPOOL

When Beethoven's fourth piano concerto was first
performed the audience was, by some accounts, deeply
shocked. Ignoring the convention by which the solo
instrument sits quietly for a few minutes while the
orchestra introduces the opening subject, Beethoven,
unable to wait, plunged straight in with the piano. Actually,
plunged is the wrong word since the piano begins with a
kind of ruminative murmur, as if unaware of the orchestra
and the frozen audience. The orchestra, apparently taken
aback by the piano's still self-absorption, repeats the
soloist's phrase but in a different key. Much of the frisson
this undoubtedly caused at the time has been diluted by
our musical sophistication; there's not much a composer
can do these days which can surprise us in the same way,
but there are times when the concerto still has the power
to lift the listener clear of his body and float him shivering
in space for a time. It relates to nothing one knows or
understands; it seems to equate to the essence of the
unknown, a numbing experience which leads one through
a series of related moods which, for no explicable reason,
grasp one's very soul. It has perhaps the hallucinatory
quality of an acid trip except that here one sees nothing
and feels everything.

That, at any rate, was how it was for Andrew. He had
come to the concert not for the pleasure of hearing the
music but for the pain of seeing Lesley's violinist. Yet

again, he had no option but to admire Lesley's taste. She was a very pretty young woman with, indeed, wonderfully supple biceps which flexed seductively beneath the gauzy sleeves of her black dress as the orchestra sawed happily through the Mozart overture. He remembered with a pulse of regret the firm muscles on the inside of Lesley's thigh and cursed himself for being so damned reasonable. He wanted to hate the fiddler and find her physically repulsive. It was typical that, when he badly needed something to kick against, he found himself effortlessly approving Lesley's choice and sympathising with the difficulties which she would face in pursuing their affair.

He broke off his thoughts as the conductor reappeared, ushering in the soloist who stumbled lankily behind his magisterial leader. Andrew breathed in during that marvellous pause before the baton drops and then the opening folded him in its intense meditation, drawing him away into a conversation which, while not wholly intelligible, had an unarguable and urgent relevance. The conductor exuded bearded, benign confidence waving languidly at the basses, nodding at the oboes. The pianist was drugged, away in a demonic land, fighting an agonised battle whose outcome, even whose purpose, was uncertain. The only means for his release and salvation was the piano he alternately caressed and ravaged; it was his link with reality but, at the same time, the instrument of his madness. The conductor coaxed him, glancing with concern and reassurance over his shoulder, nursing him firmly through the purifying ordeal. Sometimes he would bend down towards the pianist and look deep and lovingly into the glazed eyes of the hunched puppet.

At the first cadenza, instead of swimming gently out into the precise harmonies of Beethoven's familiar notes, the soloist swept himself away on an opaque storm-sea of his own creation, floundering for a time but at length resolving the confusion, ordering the hectic notes and coming at last miraculously to rest, reuniting himself with the orchestra with the quiet inevitability of two space ships docking in a dark void. The soloist seemed to gain confidence, not as a player, but as the soul of the work, in the sweet short, loving duet of the second movement and in the third, played expansively with the orchestra, echoing a phrase, mischievously picking it up and tossing it in the air. As he finished, he tottered off the platform as if at the end of an arduous self-inquisition, returning wanderingly to bow, ostensibly to the audience but in reality to the maestro who had been his companion on the journey and brought them both safely home. Andrew saw them both bending low over each other's hands as if to kiss them in homage.

In due course they motored smoothly past the ancient Turkish fishing boats into the little marina at Tsarevo – very much in line with George's expectation of the idyllic Black Sea tourist trap. After Peter had made fast he told George to relax onboard while he went to make contact with Milena. George was happy enough to pour himself a beer and sit in the shade on deck. He pottered about looking for something to read but found nothing. Clearly Peter's charterers were either illiterate or brought their own books. He had no scruples about poking his head round the door of Peter's cabin. He saw nothing to interest him beyond a battered copy of L'Express and a copy of the Times. He picked up the magazine; the words might mean nothing but at least it had pictures and, with luck, pictures of a good-looking model or two. He was dozing over it in his chair when Peter hailed him from the quayside.

"Hey, George, man. Come and say hello to Milena."

He stood up blearily and walked across to the side of the deck. On the quay stood Peter, holding a fat round loaf of bread under his arm and a bottle of wine in each hand. Beside him stood a girl whose appearance made George's heart sink. Oh, dear Christ, he thought, how am I going to live onboard next to that? She was exactly like the models in Peter's magazine. Not just pretty but heart-lurchingly stylish. She had short, very dark brown hair in what George thought of as a boy's haircut although, come to think of it, he had never seen any boy with hair like that. Her face was dramatically pale (it must be make-up surely? Her lips seemed to be white too), strong, thin eyebrows and she was wearing a bright red shirt-dress of startling shortness. George gazed at the brown legs which poured endlessly down from it and at the brown shoulder creaming from the top. Who was the prat who said it looked even better on a man?

Peter and Milena climbed aboard and she held out her hand to him.

"Hello, George," she said in a Gina Lollobrigida sort of voice. "I'm very pleased to meet you. I hope you don't mind if I come to share the boat with you."

"Delighted," muttered George, shuffling backwards to give her room and forcing himself to look into her eyes. Could they tell from the position of your eyeballs if you looked at their breasts? Did they mind? Could they blame him, for heaven's sake, if they insisted on dressing like that? My God, she didn't seem to have much on under the shirt. He'd heard about bra-burning and had the impression that girls in London didn't go in for corsets much these days but there hadn't been much evidence of it in Beirut. There was no shortage of mini-skirts but nothing like this. And she smelled wonderful too.

They sat down and Peter poured more beers. George still felt uneasy. He had little experience of women and certainly none of women like this. He had no idea how to behave or what to say to her. All he could think about was the astonishing body so much of which was now stretching itself languidly in the chair beside him and the rest of which he dared not think about, hiding not very well beneath the shirt. He stared at the deck to be on the safe side. He felt almost angry; it wasn't fair that so much excitement should be put in front of him when he was in no position to do anything about it even if he had known what to do. He almost wished she'd go away. He supposed gloomily that Peter was… well he'd find out soon enough. He was conscious that Peter had said something to him and that Milena was looking sideways at him from under her dark bob.

"Sorry, chum, miles away. Say again."

"I just asked if you'd mind being left on your own this afternoon for a bit. I've got to check out a couple of potential contacts, you know…" He waggled his hands flat in front of him in a mock-conspiratorial way. "Can you take charge of the boat till I get back, hey?"

"No trouble," said George flatly. He couldn't decide whether he was glad to be on his own again or sad because Milena was going. "You carry on. I'll be ok. Not likely to go sailing off anywhere much."

Peter laughed. "Perhaps better if you didn't. Anyway, you'll have Milena to talk to; she's chattier than me."

George's heart did its sinking thing again.

"Oh, isn't she..? aren't you..? isn't she..?"

"No, I think it's better that she should stay on board, out of sight, okay? If we are seen going round together, well you never know, walls have eyes. So, see you later. Milena will make you a terrific meal. She cooks in five languages too. Don't wait for me. I may be quite late."

He swung over the rail and jumped lightly down onto the pontoon.

"So long, Milena. Look after him, hey?"

George sat down again and picked up his beer. He smiled nervously at Milena and gazed out in what he hoped was an inoffensive but neutral way out over the marina.

"Nice chap, Peter," he said.

"Yes, I like him ver much," said Milena. "He is ver good at his job."

"Known him a long time, I expect?"

"Yes, I have know him for three years. But I have only seen him perhaps four times in all that time."

"Only four times?"

"Oh, yes. We meet only when business makes us. Not more."

"I rather got the impression you were very old friends."

"No not especially friends, He is a colleague but he's a what you call it? Acquaintance? I don't know him well at all. And he keeps himself ver much to himself. He doesn't talk much."

"I'd noticed."

"I find it hard to feel relaxed with a man who doesn't talk. I feel they are, what? Buttoned up in their coats. It is a ver

English characteristic, I think."

"Probably right," said George swallowing. "Depends a bit on the company of course. You know, who you're with."

"You are right, of course," she said. It is so important to have two people in harmony to make conversation, just as to make love."

She crossed her legs. George swallowed again and looked deep into his glass. She put a hand on his arm. "I think you are not very English. You have a sort of European air. Do you live in England?"

"No, not for years," he said. "Been in Beirut for the last eight."

"Well, so I was right." She laughed and threw her head back. George thought it was all right to look at her throat so long as it went no further. It was worth it.

"So you are a man of the Mediterranean, you are a Latin! Beirut, such style it has. Such élégance." She pronounced it the French way which didn't surprise him It seemed entirely appropriate that she should.

So you are a Latin," she went on. "A romantic no doubt."

"Hard to say really. I've never given it much thought. Pretty bog-standard English I'd say."

"But I am every fond of people," he added without meaning to. "I'm always happier when I've got people round me. Better in company."

"Of course you are. I can tell that you have warmth. You are a good listener."

"Have to be in my job," he said, convincing himself. "Wine trade, lots of customers coming in to sample bottles. You've got to keep the blighters happy and listen to their chat so they feel you're a good chap to buy hooch off."

"Of course. I knew it."

She stood up suddenly. "I would like to take my bag down to the cabin now. Will you show me the way?"

"Delighted," said George, getting up too. "Allow me," he added picking up her case with a daring touch of gallantry. He felt he could risk a certain facetiousness now they seemed to be on reasonable terms.

"Not sure what the arrangements are," he said as he led the way down the short ladder. "I'll put it in Peter's cabin, shall I?"

"For the moment. Thank you."

He put the case inside the door and stood aside to let her pass.

She went to the porthole and looked out.

"It's ver beautiful. Even more beautiful through the window," she said. "Ver romantic the Black Sea."

"Pretty good, isn't it?" he agreed.

"Come and look," she said, "What sort of bird is that out there?"

He squeezed past her case and peered out of the porthole. She was very close to him; he could feel the warmth of her bare arm on his. His head swam for a moment.

"Where are we looking?" he asked. "Oh it's just flown away," she said. "Never mind, it will come back." There was a slight pause as they both stared at the featureless sea.

"Would you shut the door please, George?" she said still looking out of the window. "I can smell the engine from here and I don't like the fumes."

George picked his way back to the door. He had intended to go through it and back on deck out of harm's way but the touch of her skin and their comparative intimacy changed his mind. Why go now just when they were beginning to get along? He closed the door and turned back.

She was sitting on the bunk, her legs crossed, and she was undoing the second button of her dress.

"I believe for a moment you were about to desert me," she said frowning. "Don't you want to stay and talk to me? Am I boring you?"

She undid the third button. George noted that there were three more.

"Not at all," he muttered, trying to lean casually against the bulkhead. It meant that he had to bend his knees slightly to avoid banging his head on the ceiling or whatever ships' ceilings were called. The effect was to put his knee joints under terrific stress; his thigh muscles developed a twitch and his knees began to shake. The vibration transferred itself to his voice as he tried to speak. "Thought you might appreciate some time alone, that's all."

"Alone? Why? I spend so much time alone. I like to be with a man. Peter is always away. Like now. Who knows how long before he comes back?"

It was time for the fourth button.

"I don't like to feel so buttoned up," she said solemnly. With a gesture of leisurely impatience she wriggled her shoulders. This somehow seemed to make her dress fall off them. George realised that he had been right about the bra. He gazed at her, conscious of as many as three sensations. His shaking knees, now drumming a Hottentot tattoo on the bulkhead, the apparent loss of feeling in his arms and chest and the little ripple of drool making its way from his slackened jaw towards his shirt.

"George. Don't play with me," she said reproachfully. "We are both grown-ups now. Why don't you be not buttoned up too, mm? Don't you want to?"

George licked his lips again, more noisily than he intended. Slurping, he straightened up and began to feel his way across the tiny cabin towards her. Now, making no attempt to keep his eyes on her face, he fixed his eyes on her breasts as a fogbound sailor fixes a lighthouse. He had time to notice how dark her nipples were, almost chocolate, and quite small, not like the tap-handles on the ruined Roman statues at home, about the only naked breasts he'd ever got close to.

"Come, George," she murmured. "Come and sit here."

He was two paces from her. His arms stretched out stiffly following the guiding beam of his eyes. The fifth button came and went, and the dress fell to her hips. Dark hollows beckoned from its depths. Her own mouth was slightly open but her eyes were heavy, half-closed. For a moment they widened, their focus hazy, gazing apparently just over his shoulder.

"That's good," she said with a smile. "Now." And everything went black.

At home that night Andrew had sat down at his typewriter. Since it seemed likely that his affair with Lesley had ended even before it began, perhaps he could take his mind off it for a moment by pushing on with this Middle Eastern escape. He had enough cuttings now to try to establish some kind of structure: an assortment of misshapen bones on which to graft some flesh. But, if he was honest, while devising the plot would be an intriguing puzzle, he was more excited by the act of writing, inventing people and their histories, imagining the locations. A little mild erotica might also temper the nostalgia for this most elusive of women.

Thinking about it afterwards he was sorry that he hadn't been more gallant, hadn't worried more about Milena's safety, instead of howling in terror as the bag came over his head. In fact, his first reaction had been of frustration; no, that was the second; his first was puzzlement that this unwonted and unprecedented sexual excitement seemed to have made him black out. When he realised he was still awake the frustration roared in. It was absolutely bloody maddening to know that that astonishing woman was taking her clothes off barely inches away and not to be able to see her. The realisation a second later that not only was he blind but that his arms seemed to be pinioned, produced the terror. Someone else was in the room, unknown and unsuspected, like the bogeyman his mother had always warned him would come and get him if he wasn't good. He hadn't been bad, he hadn't had the chance, he was just escorting a young lady to her cabin. He hadn't done anything, he heard himself yelling as he struggled furiously with the rope that the bogeyman was now tying round his wrists.

"You be quiet, man, or I shoot you," said a man's voice in his right ear. A hard finger pressed into the back of his head. "If you make noise this gun make you quiet, okay?" The finger transformed itself at once into the small black hole at the end of a silencer. As it pressed into his neck George could feel that circle of flesh being drawn inexorably into the hole as if inviting the bullet to meet it halfway. He could see it rushing up the narrow tube exploding into his skull like a sky-rocket with a million brilliant lights. To his own surprise he fell absolutely silent but for the jangling in his head and the tortured gargle of his breathing.

"Good man," said the voice. "Now we go."

George felt himself being turned and pushed back up the steep ladder to the cockpit. He heaved himself panting onto the deck, collapsed on all fours like an ageing St Bernard.

"Come, man," said the voice. "Now you must jump."

"Jump?" shouted George, choking himself as suddenly as the silencer (was ever an instrument so well named?) savagely invited more of his neck down its barrel. "For Christ's sake," he whispered piteously, his words fighting to escape from the stifling bag. "Don't make me jump, not with my hands tied. I'll drown."

He could feel the boat's rails pressing into the top of his thighs, could hear the sea smacking its lips along the side of the boat below.

"Climb over, man. Or my gun go bang. You not drown."

In a trance George heaved the bulk of his left leg over the rail, then his right, perching like an overweight tightrope walker, his heels digging into the gunwale. The jangling in his ears now drowned out all the other sounds and the numbness in his body meant that he didn't feel the push in his back, simply the wrenching emptiness as he fell.

The surface hit him like a sledgehammer. He lay quite

winded, on the quayside, bleeding from the mouth, groaning monstrously. His shattered mind could give him no information about whether he was alive or dead and, in either case, where he was.

After a moment his voice found him.

"Good jump. Now come."

George felt himself heaved to his feet and fed bodily onto the hot shiny plastic of a car's back seat. A door slammed, an engine roared, a lurch and then the noisy, sickening swaying of a drive at speed.

George might, possibly, have been relieved to know that Milena had not suffered the same treatment. She was now standing alone at the boat's rail, watching as the old Peugeot carried George dustily away. Idly she refastened the buttons of her red dress and smiled as a figure emerged from a warehouse on the quayside and walked slowly towards the boat.

The man swung himself easily over the rail and put his hands on her shoulders.

"Good." he said, "a perfect piece of work, hey? And so, if I may say so, are you."

"You are a nice man, Peter," she said, taking his hands in hers and guiding them to the top of her dress. "Now please you help me with these buttons."

AUGUST 27, THURSDAY
LONDON

In so far as Tenison had a heart, the larger part of it sank when he entered Q's office. Q was in his window mode, standing outlined against the pane, his arms stretching to either side of the frame, his head resting on the middle transom, like an attenuated back view of Christ. Tenison knew that this meant trouble: Q had reached, for the moment, the limit of the area where his actions were self-determining, where training, breeding and good practice meant that the machinery appraised the situation automatically, changed gear as necessary and hummed quietly towards a satisfactory resolution. Q was now having to think. Circumstances had so far changed that he was faintly surprised by their course; he was a long way from being rattled but, let's not strain our imagination, he was, he admitted to himself, a little puzzled.

"On the desk," he said out of the window as Tenison noiselessly closed the door.

Tenison saw a closely-folded copy of the Times on the desk. Indeed, beyond the wholly supererogatory blotter, that was all there was on the desk. He knew where to look. The entry had been neatly ringed by Q's secretary's Parker.

> **Q Location George/Alex rejected. Alternate Ashkabad Road Iran. 1 mile border. 3am 2 September. SKVP.**

Tenison opened his mouth to speak.

"Don't ask, dear boy, we don't know. No doubt it's something to do with their predilection for chess but I must say I find the Russians' mania for playing silly games almost trying. Ashkabad, I ask you. What's wrong with Batumi? At least you can get a meal of sorts there. I gather.

But Iran? There's nothing but desert. Especially at three in the morning. Personally I blame the Americans."

"The Americans? Surely they're not involved?"

"No, Alec. Not the CIA, the Americans. I refer to the natives, or rather the immigrants who make up the native population. You know, the people who think they're in a film all the time. Whose every reaction is conditioned by what they think Gary Cooper would say, who can't get into a car without trying to look like John Wayne. Who wear cowboy boots to the office, for God's sake. One day, you mark my words, that country will be run by B movie actors and the real joke will be that nobody even notices."

"Have you spoken to Alex?"

"No, but the second secretary in Tehran has. Since our rather fortunate, what shall I say, acquisition of Alex, the second secretary has got to know him quite well. I understand that he has enlarged his personal vocabulary by several phrases and expletives hitherto unknown even to him. Alex's language would be disgusting if I could understand it."

"He doesn't want to go?"

"He didn't want to go to the Black Sea. He certainly doesn't see the fun in the voyage of the dawn treader up the Ashkabad Road."

"Doesn't want to go home then?"

"He says he doesn't really regard Russia as home except in a political sense and, as such, doesn't much want to live there. To tell the truth I rather see his point. Just because the Soviet Union has more Muslims than the rest of the Islamic world doesn't mean to say that your average Russian has any more in common with the Muslims than you or I. Alex, being Egyptian, doesn't think he has much in common with the Muslim republics. He used to live in Leningrad. Lucky chap. It's a fine city with some remarkable paintings. If you ever get ther chance to see the work of a woman called Serebriakova, jump at it. It shows the astonishing sensuality of a race we choose too easily to classify as culturally moribund. Yes, but of course he wants to go home; he wants to get back to Egypt but he knows that I have no intention of letting him go home."

"Isn't it a bit of a risk to let him out at all?"

"It's a very considerable risk to do anything with a spy of his calibre and whom SKVP want back so very much. But, if we don't take him with us the Russians will certainly know and that puts George at considerable risk as well as us. Alex also knows that, if we do let him out on a dummy run, the Russians may try to kill him if they don't think they're going to get him back. Better that than that he should go on being a security risk."

"Are you going to agree to the change of venue?"

"Already in hand. There seemed to be little point in making a fuss. We want them to relax and the best way to do that is to make them think we're rattled and in a mood to play along. Peter will, of course, be monitoring all messages and we have to rely on his being in Iran to provide SKVP with a surprise. The plan, quite simply, is to ambush their ambush. We get George and hang on to Alex. It is therefore in everyone's interests that we appear to do what they want. Just for the sake of form however we have insisted on September the fourth."

"Any particular reason?"

"Absolutely. Partly to give Peter plenty of time to get to Ashkabad. The second was too soon and the third has unfortunate associations. I didn't want anyone accusing us of triumphalism."

AUGUST 28

The Times

> **SKVP. Agree George/Alex exchange Ashkabad Road. Insist 4 September. 3am acceptable. Q.**

George sat huddled in a corner of someone's bedroom. It wasn't a cell but a perfectly respectable, simply furnished room with a bed, complete with mattress and sheets, a wardrobe, a plain table and a picture of someone with a big moustache and a fez. Metal shutters, closed with a padlock, let in some light and less air.

There was no reason for him to sit in the corner. He could perfectly easily have sat or lain down on the bed since the rope round his wrists permitted him a certain amount of free movement.

He chose not to, partly because he felt that, since he was a prisoner, he might as well behave like one. Even if they were keeping him in a hotel it would be inappropriate for him to use the room as such. But also because he felt ashamed. He had had enough time to play over the scene of his kidnapping to remember his howling, animal panic, his utter conviction that, at long last, the bogeyman had come for him and that a humiliating and shameful end awaited him. He knew now, in the sticky quiet of his corner, that he had momentarily lost his reason. Some people would have regarded that as understandable and have been comforted that they were once again in their right minds. For George it was as if his every guilty secret, most of them previously unknown even to him, had been blazoned across the front page of every paper in the world. He felt reduced to nothing. He knew too that it was something to do with sex; after all he had always been led to believe that there was little more shameful than sexual excitement. He remembered with a shudder of puzzlement that last glimpse of café au lait breasts and moaned, gripping his arms between his knees in mortification.

The bosom he had in mind was at that moment at rest, glistening a little more perhaps, exactly where he had last seen it, in the sunny shade of the main cabin of the yacht. George's frustration would not have been lessened by the knowledge that the unabridged contents of the red dress were on show, stretching deliciously in the afternoon heat while, beside her, perhaps rather less obviously appreciative than George would have been, sprawled Peter, smiling with quiet amusement at his copy of the Times.

AUGUST 29

Peter in Beirut. Attention attention. Q.

"Well, well," he said putting down the paper and idly running a finger along the line of Milena's armpit. "We seem to have been here before. Why is it that every time you come aboard I get a message to go on duty hey?"

"Show me," she said and, rolling onto her front, picked up the paper. She exploded with laughter almost at once.

"So now Q is calling you to help him! And, for him, you are still in Beirut!" she spluttered. "Peter, I think you are such clever man. Did you know he would do that? Mm? Tell me true."

"I rather hoped something along those lines would happen," said Peter, "but I must say I didn't think it would work out quite so neatly."

He rolled in his turn onto his stomach and watched his finger explore a couple of interesting little dimples near the base of her spine.

"Anyway he's done himself a good turn, our Mr Q. I think we can save him the trouble of getting up so very early. But, since we don't have to bother about Batumi and we have a few days before we need to do anything, perhaps we'll just send a little message to Uncle Rex and then go for that cruise before it gets interrupted again, hey? What do you think?"

The dimples crinkled with pleasure.

AUGUST 31

The Times

Rex. Urgent admin Cessna 2 September Mashad.

George at Mary's. Homesick. Peter.

The phone rang beside the bath. From the green depths of

the water a hand emerged, well-manicured and wearing a large gold signet ring on its little finger.

"Yes?"

"Sorry to trouble you, Rex." It was a man's voice, quiet, respectful but confident. "Have you seen the paper this morning?"

"No. Clearly, I should."

"There's a message."

"Yes."

"Shall I read it to you?"

"Good idea."

"It's from Peter. It says 'Rex, urgent admin Cessna 2 September Mashad. George at Mary's. Homesick.'."

"Yes."

"Don't you think it's odd that Peter should message you?"

"Not at all. He knows Q is… away on business. What more natural than to refer upwards? He has, after all, apparently found out where SKVP are holding George."

"Mary's."

"Quite so."

"Do we know where Mary's actually is?"

"Yes, it's actually a town called Mary in Soviet Turkmenistan. Not much there beyond a rather grim collection of what on the face of it are admin buildings. We think it's almost certainly SKVP's HQ."

"Anything I should do?"

"Only what Peter asks. Talk to Mashad. Make certain the plane is properly fuelled and ready for him. Better be quick. There's only a day in hand."

"Very good, Rex."

"Goodbye. Thank you for calling."

The receiver was replaced in its cradle. The elegant hand stretched forward and began to toy with the edge of a toenail; the expensive varnish was beginning to chip.

In his corner George's worm was beginning to turn. While he refused still to sit anywhere but in the hard angle of the walls, there was now something defiant about the hunch of his shoulders; his elbows folded across his huddled knees cradled his head almost aggressively. He had, he thought, had about enough. While he had no idea why he was here, it was clear that his capture was linked with his work in Beirut and his subsequent scurry round the depressed areas of the Middle East. But this had not been part of the agreement. He had agreed, out of loyalty, to act as a passive middle-man for whatever government business they needed him for. But he remained a wine-merchant, he'd made that perfectly clear at the time. His complaisance in their skulduggery had never implied an acceptance that he would have to run, ducking and weaving, in danger of his life.

There were other people who were meant to do that and were no doubt so generously paid for it that the life they led between escapades was doubly enjoyable. His life up to now, had been acceptable, but nothing special. If they were going to start getting him killed they should bloody well have paid him rather better. And why hadn't the people who were meant to be his bosses looked after him more carefully? Where the hell was Q? Who the hell was he, for that matter? Sitting behind a bloody great desk, smoking a cigar, most likely, wholly unconcerned, indeed probably entirely unaware that he, George, was now crouched, hot, hungry and shit-scared in the corner of a no-star hotel in a hick town in Bulgaria, waiting while his kidnappers decided what to do with him. He whimpered and bit his lip at the thought of the gun pressed to the back of his head.

The door opened and George's captor came in. George knew it would be him and did not trouble to move his head. He raised his eyes slightly and took in the by now familiar figure in the shirt, jeans and incongruous red leather shoes. The man's face was obscured, as always, wrapped in a black and white keffiyeh. Not even the gleam of an eye was visible. He put a bowl of rice and a small cup of black coffee on the floor beside George.

"Good appetite," he said.

"You're too bloody kind," said George.

FIVE

LIVERPOOL

An empty Coke can skittered noisily across the path, driven by a sudden gust of dry wind. Andrew watched it pile into the ribbon of accumulated litter along the path with sour satisfaction. In the old days the park had been one of their favourite walks, big enough for privacy but without the alienating isolation of, say, the Welsh hills. Now, as reality again nudged him knowingly, it suited him once more; the contrast between earlier walks arm in arm and the polite formality of the discreet gap between them as they sauntered; the infuriating niggle of the breeze which replaced the sultry still of earlier walks; the mottled thighs beneath the short leather skirt of the fat girl who lay obliviously beside the path, submerged by a slowly-writhing mess of bomber jacket and jeans, made his mouth turn down in disgust.

Making the whole thing more elaborate, building it up like a drama, was all part of the process of making it easier for him. The more he appeared to be in a film the less chance reality had of breaking in; the longer he could go on imagining the torment of lovers about to separate, the longer he could postpone the kick in the stomach of his own desertion and despair.

The problem was that he could always see the other side of the argument. People knew this and he was used to hearing about their troubles because he could be relied on to listen and make comforting noises to boost their egos. So it was that, instead of Lesley explaining gently why she was leaving him and trying to soothe his hurt feelings, she was telling him about the problems of being gay and asking his advice about how to cope with it.

"Don't feel hurt because she's a girl," she was saying kindly. "I know men have this enormous hang-up about lesbians and often feel more threatened by them than by gay men. I suppose they somehow see it as an affront to their masculinity. 'There's nothing wrong with a lesbian that a good fuck won't put right.' I think that's how most men feel secretly."

He wanted to interrupt and to explain where she'd misjudged him but his depression had clamped his jaws in a wry smile which he failed to unlock in time to stop her sweeping on.

"But it's not such a problem," she said, well into her lecture mode. "You must have had friends at school, the boys you shared fags with behind the bike shed. No, come to think of it, you probably didn't have bike sheds at your school, behind the carports then. The friends you talked about sex with or played cricket with or whatever. You were close to them, loyal to them, if there'd been a war you might even have died for them without even thinking about it. So men can love men without wanting to roger each other. And that's the point with me. All I'm trying to say is that there are gradations of love between men and women and men and men and women and women. Affection doesn't have to be an exclusive thing. We're all different in our tastes. You generally prefer doughnuts to eclairs but have been known to eat three eclairs at the same time. I generally prefer women to men but have been known… Well that's my point. You mustn't feel threatened."

"I don't."

"Yes, you do. You said you did. But you don't need to. It's nothing personal."

"Yup," he said, shuffling savagely through the crisp packets. What he meant was no but it seemed too much of an effort to try to explain. As much as anything he felt cheated. He was the bloke being deserted; it was his life being messed around, his stomach being churned. And, instead of being allowed to indulge in a little unmitigated self-pity, he had been manoeuvred yet again into having to listen to someone else's problems and the worst part was that they were the problems of the girl who was pissing him about. Apart from taking his acquiescence entirely for granted, she was now casting him as the standard egocentric male. He felt himself to be pretty much of a new sort of man. He understood the need for women to have close personal relationships with other women. If he was honest, as he usually was, he could see that women, reacting against what they saw as the monstrous tyranny of men, would naturally find comfort in the shared ideas and aspirations of other women and that, in their natural desire to do things on their own without male interference, they might decide that even sex was more fun without a male ego in the bed.

He understood all this. He wanted to explain that it wasn't a question of feeling threatened, and that the sex of her new lover was mostly irrelevant. The problem was a much more basic one. She had a new lover, that was what mattered and he was being ditched. He couldn't have felt more pissed off if the new lover had been a Doberman pinscher. The style wasn't important. It was the substance that counted.

And yet he felt uneasy. If he really plumbed his store of honesty he knew that a fragment of his usually well-disciplined id was making a serious bid for freedom. He had been waiting at a bus-stop one night and had watched two girls through the window of an adjacent café. They were holding hands energetically across the table and their bodies moved towards each other and away again in excitement as they talked, while their four hands were locked over the salt cellar as if it were an anchor. Through the smeared glass and framed by a mocking curtain of tired red gingham they had been an unsuspecting sideshow. Roll up and see the lesbian ladies! Sixpence to hear them talk dirty to each other! He had seen them again a little later after they came out and huddled together in the twilit bus shelter. They both wore similar light-coloured raincoats and they might have been sisters, perhaps that was their story as, with arms tightly linked they stared out at the drizzling mist. Every now and then they tentatively exchanged the despairing kisses of people guiltily in love, each kiss more tormentingly addictive and each more nearly fatal. Andrew had felt a great wave of sympathy and sadness for them. Had they nowhere to go? Were they reduced to this desperate and furtive lovemaking in shabby shelters? At the same time he knew that his sympathy was not wholly innocent. He had enjoyed watching them. It was in no sense titillating but, in some vicarious way, he had shared their passion.

"So it's not easy for us," Lesley was saying. Thirty years ago they'd have put us in a loony bin."

"Then why do it?" he longed to shout. "Why give up the modest excitements of a love affair with me for all that. It won't even last once the sex has worn off." But he didn't.

"I know," he said. "You're going to have a tough time. I'm sorry for you. "But it'll be worth it if you really care for each other."

He picked up a discarded can and threw it easily at a waste-bin. It missed and tumbled onto the grass. A man in his thirties in a leather jacket was cycling past.

"Don't chuck it on the grass," he shouted. "There's a perfectly good bin over there."

And when you leave me
I know you'll grieve me

The sun sets around six o'clock in the southern Black Sea once summer begins to wane and the life goes out of it a little; the temperature may rise only as high as the low thirties on a bad day.

While of undisputed interest to the casual tourist thinking of spending a week or so in the region, these meteorological facts would matter less to those who spend most of their lives there. For them the sun rises, becomes tolerably or intolerably hot, and then sets. It is not something they notice. Apart from those who live by the land the weather is generally only noticed by inhabitants of countries where it is habitually bad. The English talk daily about the weather; Sicilians do not.

Even had the isobars in the Black Sea suddenly adjusted themselves to reproduce the first August rain storm since records began however, it is unlikely that Peter or Milena would have noticed. They had rediscovered an altogether more intriguing way of passing the time and were so deeply absorbed in it that the first they would have known of the great Flood would have been the moment the earth moved as they grounded on Ararat. As it happened Peter's interest was one which George shared, although, in comparison, George's was a rather rougher, more amateurish approach. He would have at once envied Peter's opportunity to pursue his passion and admired the whole-hearted commitment which he brought to it: the exhaustive but (and here George's absence was a bonus) leisurely exploration of the finer features of Milena's physique. She was, as George had had time to notice, beautifully made, and Peter was an appreciative connoisseur. But it should be said that, as with all great cultural endeavours, the connoisseur gave as much as he took. Peter was himself a figure of some stature, handsomely chiselled, with a stomach like a washboard and that crinkly fair hair which, as people like George know, not only never loses its style but also never grows on the heads of people like George. So Milena, I think, was not dissatisfied; there was a harmonious balance in the yacht's cabin. They were, George would have had to admit, a better-matched couple than if it had been him in Peter's place. And handsome too, an aesthetically pleasing contrast of bronzes and browns, smooth as hand-carved wood, slipping sensually in and out of shadow, limb intertwined with limb in a purposeful dance of desire.

I have in my mind as it were a series of photographs of this dance, artfully framed like publicity stills, each a frozen moment hinting at the excitement of the whole performance. In one of those stills Peter is lying on his back, his blond head clear against the white sheet, while diagonally across him, belly to belly, face down, her dark hair framing her face sprawls Milena. Down the dark crease of her spine gleams a smear of sweat. Because it's a still no one is moving but I can hear a voice from the blond head.

"George," it says.

SEPTEMBER 1

It was only when he heard the running footsteps that George realised that the two sharp cracks had been gun shots. He flung himself sideways, trying to wriggle under the bed, but his cramped knees and shortness of breath meant that only his head had reached cover by the time the door burst open.

He lay motionless, knowing the futility of movement, waiting for whatever was to happen. Perhaps they were at long last going to shoot him. To his surprise he didn't even terribly mind; it would at least be a positive action, an end to the timeless limbo in which he had been suspended since… when? He had no longer a clear idea of time. He had no clear idea of anything beyond that it was somehow easier to lie panting on the floor, looking at his body spread beside him and to wait for someone else to make a decision.

"Playing the ostrich, hey, George?" said a familiar voice.

"Just because you can't see me doesn't mean I can't see you, you know. Come on out, we should be moving."

George moved his head to change his point of view. He saw a pair of brown hairy legs wearing desert boots. They moved slightly as a face loomed hugely towards him.

"Come on, George. We shouldn't waste time."

"Peter."

"That's me. Sorry it took so long to find you."

George found it hard to speak; his throat was constricted

by a great gag of sentiment and he seemed to have lost the habit of articulate speech. Peter helped him gently to his feet and, with an arm round his waist, guided him through the door. George hesitated as they entered the corridor but Peter, sensing his thoughts, reassured him.

"It's ok, George. They've gone. No more trouble now."

"Did you kill them?"

"No need. They ran off as soon as they saw me. I just fired over their heads as they ran. Only chancers. Just boys. You must have got used to that in Beirut."

"Well I heard it happened. First time I've actually experienced it."

They went down in the lift to the lobby, a poky hallway which smelled of sweat and ghaz.

"How did you know where to find me?"

"I asked around. It's surprising how much people know and the kidnap of a European isn't likely to be a secret for long."
"Who were they?

"Chancers, as I say. Amateurs. But probably put up to it by someone."

"Palestinians?"

"Possibly."

"Who else would it have been?"

"Who can tell? Peter had flagged down a badly-rusting Peugeot taxi and they got in. If he had looked behind him, George would have noticed a young man standing by the hotel entrance quietly raise a hand as if in farewell. Since George had never seen his face he would not have recognised it. But the red shoes might have been familiar.

Andrew's knowledge of the Eastern Mediterranean was at best hazy and he had spent an enjoyable hour in the local library leafing through large scale maps of the area. Where was Ashkabad, how was Peter going to get there and how long would it take? It might call for some imagination on both their parts.

SEPTEMBER 1

The Times

Peter in Iran. Flight booked ETA 2 am 2 Sept.

Koppeh Dagh EZW106. Rex.

"So they made you swim to the side?" asked Peter.

"No such luck, old boy," replied George. "They more or less pushed me off the side onto the quay. One moment I thought I was going to drown, the next wallop! There was I flat on my face in the dust. I can tell you I was so surprised to be alive I didn't even feel the pain. Not until later anyway. I must have hit the ground quite a crack. You can probably see the dent in the quay if you look."

He took a long swig of the whisky Peter had poured him. For once it was what he wanted.

They were sitting on deck near the stern, looking out into the hazy twilight of the Bulgarian waters as they headed back towards Istanbul. In the taxi Peter had explained

SKVP's rejection of the Batumi rv and they had driven straight back to the boat where Milena, wearing a yellow Snoopy t-shirt, had greeted George warmly. She kissed him lovingly on each cheek and, looking deep into his eyes, winked elaborately as if to say "Our little secret, no?"

"I am so sorry, George," she said huskily. "They came so suddenly, it was so fast."

"No worry, old thing. Not your fault. These things happen."

Now Peter smiled gently as he listened to George's story.

"And what next?" he asked quietly. "They put you in a taxi, I guess?"

"Some sort of car, yes. Just stuffed me in the back. Of course I'd no idea where we were going with a bloody bag over my head. To be honest I couldn't have cared much either. I was about as frightened as I've ever been. The only thing I hung on to was the thought that the longer they didn't shoot me, the less likely they were to do so. Whoever they were. You said you thought they were amateurs, didn't you?"

"Possible. Maybe probably. You know from your own experiences in Beirut that there are plenty of young hoodlums who think they'll have a go at the kidnapping game, partly for the excitement, partly in the hope of quick money. As you also know, most of them end with everyone dead, including the hostage. You were lucky, George."

"I suppose so. Don't want to sound ungrateful but I didn't feel particularly lucky at the time. The really spooky thing was that one or other of us always had his head in a bag. Me literally and then, when we got there, they always had a keffiyeh or something round their faces. It was like talking to a ghost."

"They didn't want to be identified, obviously."

"I know why they wore them, for God's sake," said George irritably. "I'm just saying it made the whole thing even weirder."

"I feel very bad that it happened at all. I can't tell you how badly I feel about it. I had no idea it would happen here. Turkey, Syria, Lebanon, sure but Bulgaria?"

"Not your fault, old boy," said George magnanimously. "You weren't to know a bunch of cowboys were going to try their luck."

"If they were cowboys."

"I thought you were sure they were."

"Not sure. It's likely. But not definite. I have to admit there are certain aspects of the administration of your section which worry me a little."

"I've always been on time with my rvs and drops. Well pretty much always."

"No, I don't mean your end of it. I'm thinking about the London end."

"Anything special?"

"No, but there's been an accumulation of little things which make me uneasy. The whole business of your departure from Beirut was frankly a mess, for instance. Then I think it was very unwise to make so public that you were in Istanbul when you were obviously on the run. I just wonder how much importance Q attaches to your well-being." He stopped.

"Well not a lot obviously. But, God, are you saying he's deliberately trying to get me bumped off?"

"No, not that otherwise he would have had you killed by now. I can't put my finger on it but I have to say I've my doubts about his reliability. But that's just me. I'm a born sceptic. Don't worry about it."

There was, of course, nothing he could have said more calculated to make George do just that.

Despite the comparative comfort of his bunk compared with the floor in the hotel room where he had insisted on sleeping during his captivity, George did not sleep well. He'd always thought Q a bit of an odd fish. Even though he'd never met him, something of his remoteness, his pedantic way of speaking, his lack of personal warmth had come through in his messages and in what he'd heard about him from the few people who had had dealings with him. He knew he wasn't Q's favourite agent, wasn't the chilly public school type, but he'd always, well until recently, believed that there was an unwritten rule of loyalty to the firm which worked downwards as well as upwards. The workers did their damnedest in the field and the men driving the desks, the best of whom had been in the field themselves, made certain they got all the support they needed. Of course this was the natural, generalised grousing of the poor bloody infantry about the staff johnnies safely back at HQ. He knew that most of his grumbling about Q had been no more than the sort of self-justification of the front-liner who feels his efforts aren't fully appreciated. Nonetheless, now he came to think about it, there had been a few times recently when he hadn't felt so confident about the back-up in London and even wondered what it would take to make Q drop him altogether. Not much probably, he thought. Of course, if anyone in London had ever given him the slightest clue as to how he fitted into the organisation and the end result of what he was doing, it might be easier to do it better. He felt his heart thump angrily. Christ, he could have been killed two or three times in the last week or so and Q either knew nothing or, if he did know, cared nothing or, if he cared, cared only that George should cease to be a problem.

The graceless ingratitude of the man upset George more than the thought of dying, to which he had grown curiously inured. But had Q really gone so far as to wish George dead or was it just part of his Olympian exercise of the arms' length principle?

At last the whisky took him off and sped him off to a fretful dream in which Milena, wearing the t-shirt over her head, quizzed him angrily about the names of hotels in Istanbul.

SEPTEMBER 2

His sense of foreboding was not helped the next morning by his hangover (a week on the wagon sets your resistance back by months) nor by Peter's announcement that he needed to leave George on his own since he had some business in town. "Just some routine paperwork about the boat and our visa. Milena's coming too." He looked hard at George. "I don't know how safe she'd be if I left her alone with you again." George spluttered but Peter smiled. "Don't worry, I trust you. And you'll be quite safe on board this time. Have a look over there. George squinted blearily at the quayside and saw, beside the boat, a young man who, when Peter whistled, turned and waved, grinning cheerily. It was well that he had remembered

Peter's instruction to drop the red shoes. "He'll be watching the boat." Peter was reassuring. "We shan't be long anyway. Help yourself to what you need. Have a shower or whatever. Back by lunch for sure."

George opted for the whatever in the form of the whisky bottle. He'd noticed that there was a reasonable supply in the forward storage area so saw no harm in a slightly earlier start than usual. There was no wine and, in any case, he had a week to catch up on. Wandering back towards the cockpit he paused by the chart table and stared at the radio and navigation system. It meant nothing to him but he gazed at it dimly as if the sheer force of looking might somehow make some of it clear to him. At the edge of the table were a number of notebooks and a few scraps of paper on which Peter had jotted numbers, presumably grid references or sextant readings. In the very middle of the desk was a sheaf of papers, held by a bulldog clip. George could hardly have avoided seeing it. On the top sheet someone had written a simple message as for a telegram.

"For Sept 3. Q in Iran. George left Mary's in a hurry. Hold Alex."

George leant against the doorway. This must be Peter's latest message to Q via the usual channels. He glanced at the calendar: September 2. So this was tomorrow's message. Funny that Peter hadn't mentioned it. He wondered what Mary's was. Some sort of code presumably which he hadn't come across before. He turned the sheet back to the preceding page which carried a similar message in the same writing.

"For Aug 31 Rex Urgent admin Cessna 2 September Mashad. George at Mary's. Homesick. Peter."

Rex, eh? Right to the top for old Peter. George wondered

why Peter seemed to have bypassed Q. He found his answer on the next page back.

"Q location George/Alex exchange rejected. Alternate Ashkabad road Iran. 1 mile border 3am 2 September. SKVP."

George walked away from the table to the whisky. He brought the bottle back and sitting down heavily, filled the tumbler. He took a long eye-watering pull. SKVP eh? That was a facer. That was the Russian lot, he was pretty sure. How the hell did they come into all this? And what was all this about an exchange between him and Alex, whoever he was? More to the point, why was this message, apparently from SKVP, in what – he compared it quickly with the other papers on the chart-table – was clearly Peter's writing? He turned back another page.

"Q. George now our guest," he read. "Will exchange for Alex within 8 days. Signify agreement. SKVP."

Another long swig of scotch helped his memory race through the last two weeks. August 24th had been a Monday, hadn't it? A glance at the calendar confirmed it. Of course, it had been the first Monday he'd spent on this ruddy boat. In which case – it hit with him the force of the hair of the dog – Christ. Whose guest had he been on the 24th? Peter's. In which case, he made himself say very slowly, in which case, Peter and SKVP were the same thing.

He slumped forward and let his cheek rest on the cool blue and yellow paper of the chart. He closed his eyes and tried to forget everything he'd ever known. If he tried ever so hard he might with luck wake up in his shabby but loveable room in Beirut and find it had been even more of a dream than Milena.

After a few moments he realised that, like Milena, the harsher reality was more durable than his wishes and he sat up. Appreciation of the situation, he remembered from his National Service days. Where are we? On a boat in the Black Sea. What is our strength? One. Not very fit and not very happy, but one anyway. What is our objective? To get off this bloody boat before it gets more complicated. What is our enemy's strength? God knows, could be hundreds. More to the point his real strength is that he knows more than I do. Or did. Now, at least, I know something he doesn't know I know. I am better informed in that, while I used to think he and I were working for the same people, I now know that we aren't. What are our options? Good question. I get off this boat… no, but, of course I'm not going to get off because the friendly bloke down there keeping the hoodlums out is also keeping me in. Anyway, doesn't matter. What, as I was about to say, would I be able to do if I did got out? Bugger all. I'm skint, knackered, don't speak the lingo and, in any case, haven't got anywhere to go. So option one, to leave, is aborted. Option two, to stay, seems a reasonable alternative. We can assume, for the purposes of this appreciation, that George's new first rule of survival applies: if he hasn't killed me yet, he probably doesn't need to. Why not? Because I'm either no threat or can be some use to him. What use? Another good question. Answer, of course, I'm a swap for Alex. Best way to find out? Ask him.

A thought: if you confront him with what you've found, you will have given away the only card you have. Thought two: may he not (a) be less than pleased and (b) feel that he has to get rid of you? Another cracker, God you're on good form. Answer, quite possibly. On the other hand (a) he didn't exactly hide the messages, did he? Perhaps he wanted me to see them. Why? Only Peter can tell. Another reason to ask him. And the answer to the question about being got rid of is similarly, quite possibly. He may decide you're a risk. On the other hand, if his motive for not killing you is to make use of you, killing you isn't going to help him much. After all, what can you do with the knowledge you now have? Answer, not a lot. Good point, George, got your drift. Another drink? Don't mind if I do.

When, two hours later, Peter and Milena came back aboard they found George slumped over the chart table, deep in stertorous sleep, his head resting on the sheaf of messages, now slightly dampened by the trickle of saliva from the corner of his mouth. They left him there while they sliced salad and fruit for lunch. When George awoke, half an hour or so later, and heard them, on deck, he realised quite rapidly that his options had been reduced and that he had lost the chance of introducing the matter of his discovery in his own time. He found a bottle of mineral water, went forward for a pee and, with a lumbering but curiously purposeful feeling of confidence, went up on deck.

Milena, he noticed with his usual acuity, was wearing what he could only describe as a couple of belts, matching strips of green material across her chest and hips. She was eating a peach whose juice dribbled occasionally on to her brown skin; it looked, he thought, almost like cannibalism. Peter greeted him affably. "George, man, come and have some lunch. We didn't want to disturb you, you looked so sound asleep." He pulled a chair across with his foot. "I see you found some interesting reading matter."

George helped himself to a banana. He didn't care much for bananas, monkey food he called them, but he needed something to do with his hands. He peeled it slowly, playing with it like an Arab with his worry beads. He wondered if he would ever learn that he was never at his best when woken from a drink-induced siesta.

"Yes," he said. "Look, I'm not much of a diplomat so I'm going to have to keep this awfully simple. I'm not going to apologise for reading your messages because they were there on the chart-table in full view. Either you'd forgotten to put them away which, the more I think about it, seems unlikely. Not your style. Or, which seems increasingly likely, you wanted me to find them."

Peter said nothing but inclined his head in what might have been a sign of agreement.

George went on.

"Having read the messages I draw one simple conclusion which is that you aren't, after all, working for quite the same people as I am. Now, having thought about it, that seems fair enough. I've never asked you if you were on our side and you've never claimed you were. I've simply made assumptions. I realise now that that was bloody silly."

Without thinking, he bit into the banana, filling his mouth with the moist fibrous sweetness. He gagged and coughed, spitting particles of banana over his shirt and trousers. Peter jumped up and moved over to him to pat him on the back. George waved him away.

"I'm perfectly all right, thanks. Thanks," he said firmly but thickly. "Went down the wrong way. Bit early for lunch for me." He swallowed the last of the cloying mouthful. "Not a lot more to say, really. Except that I'd seem to be pretty much without a game plan now. I'd been assuming that you were acting in loco Q and would, in due course, let me know what I was supposed to do and when I could get back to Beirut. Since I've assumed wrongly on that one too, all I can do is ask you if you're prepared to tell me who you are and what you propose to do."

Peter was pushing a glass of orange round the table. Now he looked up.

"I think that's very fair, man. Let me say one or two things before I decide how to answer what you have just said. First, I've had time to get to know you a little since you've been on this boat. I confess that I have played with you a little; well, you know that now, since you've discovered that I'm not exactly who you thought I was. And I've come to admire you a little. I think you are above all honest and surprisingly loyal. I admit that I had not intended to tell you the truth. In fact I hadn't intended to tell you anything. But I will do so because I think you deserve it.

"First then. You are both right and wrong in your conclusions, I am Peter and I am who you thought I was. I am the Peter who has been working for Q for five years and who you will have heard of as the man with the roving Middle East brief. But I am not quite the Peter everybody thinks I am. I have to explain that I value loyalty, as I said, but loyalty to causes far above people. People are expendable, they change and decay, their value varies and, usually, in the end, expires. I worked for Q not because I admired him; I only met him twice."

"More than I ever did," said George.

"Exactly. He was a man who expected not personal loyalty but loyalty to the cause."

"Which is? I've always been a bit vague on that one."

"It comes down to the preservation of peace in the Middle East, nothing more or less. Grandiose, I admit, but I suppose you could say we're the counterpart to the CIA. They go around infiltrating governments in the hope of destabilising regimes they don't much like, while we do what we can to keep government stable. Wars, however well-intentioned, cost lives and money and seldom solve any problems, even in the short term. I believe in the process of evolution. It may take longer but it's organic and its effects last longer because of it. The best revolutions come about because people have had time to digest the facts and to act with a collective will. All we aspire to do is to provide them with the facts. I admit it's a utopian, certainly Sisyphean task, but that's what ideals and causes are all about."

"The pen is mightier and all that?"

"You have it in one. Anyway I hope we will have plenty of opportunity to discuss the cause and my ideals, and perhaps yours if you will share them, but I would like to pursue what I was saying about Q. As you know, I think, he is a man who inspires little affection and does not seek it. For him the cause was what mattered. I say was because – and this will explain quite a lot to you – I have increasingly serious doubts about his commitment to the ideals which we all once worked towards. You know yourself how important it is for administrators to spend some time in the field at regular intervals to keep them in touch with the sharp end of what they're running. Q has bluntly lost touch. He has grown too used to sitting behind a desk, pulling strings, pushing pieces about on a board. What is worse is that he has begun to get careless. I told you that I valued the cause more than people. But I still value human life highly and, while I agree that it is sometimes necessary to dispose of people who are inimical to the progress of our work, I cannot bear to see life wasted. Q's careless mistakes have been responsible for the death of at least three of our – his – people, and I can see the danger of more occurring. Including, if I'm honest, your own. I'll explain that in a moment."

Peter stood up and walked over to the seaward rail. He gazed out into the brilliant dazzle of the sea.

"What I've told you so far does not, I imagine, shock you particularly. You may agree with some of it and at least understand what you don't agree with."

"That's pretty fair."

"You won't like the next bit so much, I'm afraid. You have read about Major Mike Hoare and his work in the Congo, no doubt? He is what the papers call a mercenary. He describes himself as a soldier of fortune. He is a professional fighter who will hire his skills to any side, even opposing ones. He believes in nothing but in earning a living. It doesn't matter who wins so long as he gets his bounty. I am not like Mike Hoare in any respect except one crucial one. I will work for anybody, even opposing sides, if I believe they share my ideals and ultimate ambitions."

He turned and leant his back against the rail.

"I'm a mercenary spy, George. I work for Q but I also work for SKVP as you have perhaps guessed. I am not SKVP any more than I am the Shop. As such I work for money – no, that's not quite fair, of course I am paid by my employers – but I work for ideals too. So when I see Q going wrong it worries me because it may upset all the careful balances which I have set up in my own work."

"So you're what they call a double agent?"

"Yes, if you like."

"Isn't that treachery in two directions?"

"A fair question. No, because I share my information with each side. They only know what it is necessary for them to know. And no, because I don't make a complete secret of how I work. There are people in SKVP who know that I work for the Shop."

"And you're telling me that Q knows that you work for SKVP?"

"Not Q, no. But someone higher than Q."

"And does this someone know about your doubts about Q?"

"Absolutely. It is on that person's orders that I am to do what I can to clean up Q's procedures."

"And what is that going to involve?"

"Well, for a start – I promised I would explain this to you – there is the problem of you. Your position in Beirut has been, hasn't it, essentially a sleeping one?"

"I suppose so, yes."

"What I mean is, no one has thought it worth explaining the extent of the Lebanese operation, let alone the purpose of your role."

"Good God, no. I'm just a pawn playing pass the parcel."

"Quite so. The Shop evidently regard you as extremely useful since they continue to keep you there. But you don't know why, nor what your ultimate function is."

"Not a clue. Never have."

"Nor does SKVP. But they would very much like to know. That is why they tried to kidnap you in Beirut when you were, commendably, too fast for them. I hope Q appreciates that."

"How's that going to help them?"

"Well you know the answer yourself now, since you have read the messages. Alex, whose name you read there, is an

SKVP man whom the British have been holding for nearly a month now."

George thought he remembered a report on the World Service about a spy scandal in Iran. "And SKVP want to swap Alex for me?"

"That's what they say. What they really want is to get Q out to the Middle East and kidnap him. Alex is just an excuse, he knows nothing, he's been in prison. But Q knows everything."

"Would he talk?"

"SKVP have a good record of persuading people to talk quite freely, George."

"Jesus Christ. I almost feel sorry for Q."

"Don't. Q knows the game. He has no intention of getting caught. Why should he sacrifice himself when he has you to play with?"

"Me, for Christ's sake?"

"Absolutely. You said yourself you were only a pawn. And you have the priceless benefit of knowing nothing about the organisation. You're useless to them since you can tell them nothing."

"But they don't know that."

"No, they don't."

"So what's Q's plan?"

"I don't know the details yet. I'll find out tomorrow. But you may depend on the fact that, when it comes to giving hostages to SKVP, he'll drop you without a second thought."

"But can't you tell SKVP that I know nothing?"

"No point yet. The important thing is to get Q out here. Once I know what he's planning we can take it from there. But there's something I need to ask you and you can take your time to think about your answer. I need to know your own position. If you're loyal to Q then I must find somewhere safe to drop you. Don't worry, I have no intention of having you killed. But, if you're a Q man, I must leave you out of this. On the other hand, if you take my advice – and if you trust me – you'll keep clear of Q. But that means staying here with us. It might be dangerous but your help could be invaluable. I'll leave you to think about it."

"Don't trouble. I don't need any time. You'd better count me in. Everything you've told me about Q rings true. I reckon I'm safer with you lot, although God knows what safe means these days."

Peter gripped George's shoulder.

"I'm really very glad, man. I didn't really have any doubts but I am so glad to be proved right. You were right about the messages of course. It was precisely because I felt we could rely on you that I left them there for you to find. It seemed the best way of giving you the chance to find out the truth for yourself."

"What if I'd said nothing?"

"We'd have done the same as if you wanted to stay with Q. Dropped you off somewhere."

"Thirty miles out, you mean?"

Peter laughed loudly.

"A bit closer to home than that I think."

George smiled wanly.

"Can I ask two more questions?"

"Go on."

"If it was SKVP who were after me in Beirut, who was it who really got me last week?"

"Have you any ideas yourself?"

"I've got a hunch."

"Try me."

"Well having read the messages – I mean I don't know the codes and all that – but it struck me that you might have known all along where I was. Wherever Mary's is."

"So?"

"So you might have set the whole thing up."

Peter laughed loudly. "You mean kidnap you myself?"

George hesitated. "Well, as I say, just a hunch."

"And once again you're not far wrong. We did it ourselves."

"Why, for God's sake?"

"In this business, as you know, you can never tell when you're being watched. Most of the time you just think you are but sometimes they find you. It was very important that everybody should think you'd been kidnapped, especially Q. He had to believe I was still in Beirut. If he thought you were safely with me in Istanbul all the time, he wouldn't need to fly out. It was vital that he should come, and at that stage, I didn't know whether I could afford to share that information with you."

"All right, I'll buy that." He paused. Suddenly he felt very hot all over. He glanced across to the other side of the deck. Milena, her eyes closed, was stretched out on the deck. "So… so Milena was just, just a..?"

"A lure? I'm afraid so. I'm sorry, man. Actually she's a bit of one-man girl although she likes you very much."

From the deck Milena turned her head and opened one clear green eye. She closed it slowly at George and opened it again, watching him steadily.

"Fair enough," said George. He looked out to sea for a moment.

"All right, next question. You work for the Shop and you work for SKVP. Is there, as the actress said, anyone else?"

"Do I work for any other organisation?"

"That's it."

"Who else is there?"

"I'm buggered if I know."

"Exactly."

Peter walked over to Milena and nudge her gently with his foot. "Time to get up, cara," he said. "I'll have to move soon."

"Where now?" asked George.

"You already know about the rv on the Ashkabad Road."

"God yes, I'd forgotten. Are you meant to be handing me over for Alex or something?"

"Yes, you've just been kidnapped again, George. It's getting to be a habit. You are now officially in an SKVP house in Turkmenistan. That's the dummy plan in order to get Q out. When Q knows that I've, as it were, retrieved you from the evil SKVP he will keep Alex locked up in the Tehran embassy. This is just a chance for me to meet Q and bring him to the boat for a talk. Then we shall decide what to do."

"How do you know Q is going to go to Iran? More Times messages?"

"Didn't I tell you about the short wave radio?"

"How does Q know where you are?"

"He doesn't, that's the joy of it. I'm untraceable. He can think I'm in Beirut when I'm actually in Istanbul. Easy for me to manipulate things, trickier for him."

"And you get to Iran, how?"

"There's a plane on a strip just up the coast."

"Ah, the Cessna?"

"Right. It's usually kept in Mashad. The handover was due for 2 o'clock tomorrow morning near Koppeh Dagh on the border but that was too short notice and Q has wisely insisted on Friday. And 3am, just to show who's calling the tune. It's all a bit of a charade anyway. Q thinks he's going to the Ashkabad Road but actually we've diverted him to a nice remote spot in the country pretty close to Tehran. He won't know any better. So we meet him there, make him very happy by reassuring him you're safe, then fly back with him, picking up Alex from the embassy if possible."

"And do we wait here?"

"No, you and Milena are going to take the boat to Hvar. It's a beautiful spot, almost as good as Dubrovnik, and we'll meet you there next week."

Ten minutes later, in the intimacy of the trickle from the shower, Peter ran his hands over Milena's slippery back and put his mouth against her ear.

"How did I do, carissima?" he murmured. "Not bad, hey?"

"Oh Peter, you are so clever. He believed every word."

"But he's not stupid. That was a smart question about the other organisations."

"I think he only guessing."

"You don't think," he lowered his voice to a whisper. "You don't think he somehow knows about our Israeli friends, do you?"

"Israelis? What Israelis could those be?"

He laughed loudly. "Buggered if I know."

"Milena squealed with laughter and grabbed him round the waist. "And me! I'm buggered too!"

SIX

SEPTEMBER 2, WEDNESDAY
TEHRAN

Very much to his own surprise, Q was enjoying himself. He was the sort of Englishman to whose family intercontinental travel was merely part of life. His grandfather had spent alternate years of his life travelling in China, Burma and Assam. In the years in between he would return home to father another child on his wife before leaving on his travels again shortly before the baby was born. As a result he knew his children even less well than most well-to-do Victorian fathers, although his genes were apparently dominant enough to ensure that his only son, Q's father, himself began to travel at an early age. It was Q's theory however that his father left home simply to seek out male company as a change from the governess, mother and six sisters who had hitherto ruled his life. He, by coincidence, spent much of his life in the Middle East, particularly in Persia where he had accompanied Freya Stark on her journeys remapping the long-forgotten Valley of the Assassins.

For whatever reason, Q had not inherited the strain. Travel to him meant heavy luggage, cavernously cold railway stations or extensive mal de mer. He had, in the course of his duties, flown once or twice in what he still called aeroplanes but had found it an unnatural experience, except for an unforgettable trip he had made as a young man from Poole to Alexandria by flying boat. It had taken three days, the *escales* being decided by the relationship of their fuel-supply to convenient stretches of flat water. Their first night had been spent on the lake at Biscarosse outside Bordeaux, an expanse of breathtakingly beautiful land and seascapes which, he had been pleased to learn later, had been painted once or twice by the fauve painter Marquet, a particular passion of his.

He had flown again yesterday, this time in a jet for the first time, an Air France Caravelle of such speed and comfort that he had arrived almost reluctantly in Tehran only seven hours after leaving the Dantesque turmoil of Heathrow. The Parviz hotel was on a par with anything he'd known, European food being more the norm than Persian, and he had discovered with delight the Shahanshahi Park among whose elegant arbours he was now strolling, gazing almost serenely over to the Elburz Mountains in the north where his father had himself spent so many apparently happy days. (Andrew was quite pleased to have discovered the Shahanshahi in a guide to Iran in the library. He wasn't certain about the height or proximity of the Elburz but was pretty confident that the Shah would have ensured that the park had an elegant palm house not unlike the one in Sefton Park. That, at any rate, was where Q was currently strolling.)

Q reflected that it was after all good for him to get into the field from time to time, to experience a little of what his colleagues got up to. He envied them their lot and wondered whether they appreciated the weary monotony of memoranda in triplicate and committees ad nauseam. Again to his own surprise he was less apprehensive than he had feared about the meeting tomorrow with SKVP. Or rather perhaps not with SKVP. It rather looked as if the splendid Peter had pulled not only the cat out of the bag but George, bloody George, out of the SKVP clutches. If so tomorrow's meeting would involve the release of Alex from the embassy, a debrief with Peter and then perhaps another night or two in Tehran before flying home with his charge. The only small lurking apprehension was the fact that he would be getting to the Ashkabad road by small plane and at night, but after his Caravelle flight he felt that flying held no more terrors for him. He sat on a stone bench which radiated the heat of the Persian sun and stared into the distance, almost smiling.

He would have been puzzled had he been able to see the strangely prescient message which at that moment was being set in hot metal for Thursday's Times.

SEPTEMBER 3, THURSDAY

> Q in Iran. George left Mary's in a hurry. Hold Alex.
>
> Peter.

LIVERPOOL

Andrew sat with his hand on the door handle of the red Cortina. He leaned his head sideways against the window glass trying to think of some reason not to get out. Lesley sat with her hands on the wheel, the engine running, smiling politely across at him, waiting for him to go. He knew that she wanted him to get out, wanted to drive away from him to meet her new friend. Yet he knew that, since this might be the last time ever that they sat together in her car, once he got out, the long-expected verdict would be pronounced and he would have no further claim to survive.

She had agreed to meet him earlier in the evening; he'd known she wasn't in a position to refuse him. They'd sat in a pub and talked. Or rather he'd talked and she'd listened. There wasn't a lot for her to say. There wasn't in truth much for him to say either but he managed to spin it out into endless threads of questioning, reasoning, puzzling, regretting; he went over their history, where he thought he'd gone wrong, did she agree? If not, was she sure there wasn't anything he could do? He knew about this as about everything else that there wasn't, that he was no longer a player in her game, that whatever he did from now on was of absolutely no relevance; the history of which he was part was colourful and had been fun, but history was what he was, voilà tout. Kindly, gently, repeatedly, cornily, she had explained that it was she who had changed, not him, that she was sorry but there it was, she loved Paula. Or thought she did. Maybe not, time would tell.

For you know, honey, you've had your way…

For her the evening had been a release; she had been honest but firm. There was no need to go along with his deluded perception of their relationship and, as she watched him weep, all she could feel was the urge to smile that it really was all over.

And now she waited as politely as ever for him to get out of her car and her life. He had already opened the door and put his briefcase on the pavement beside the car. It was the move which said "I'm really going now" to which she was supposed to reply, "No wait, I didn't mean it". But she didn't. She continued to wait, silently patient. She seemed for a moment to be looking over his shoulder as he began to talk again. Was she bored? No she was saying something, she was interrupting. "Please stay" did she say? No. What she said was "Briefcase" looking past him still. Turning suddenly he saw a young man loping casually away down the road carrying the briefcase with him. He was followed by another youth who was running sideways, looking back at the car.

Without a thought Andrew was out of the car and down the road, with all the furious strength that his anger, shame and wasted passion had given him. He ran like a champion. The thief sensed that he was beaten for, as he looked round to see Andrew roaring towards him like an avenging angel, he first quickened his step than, realising that he was up against a supernatural force, dropped the case contemptuously and scampered away.

Panting, Andrew reached the case and picked it up. He glanced over at the thief who was now standing on the far pavement.

"Bastard," said Andrew under his breath and began to walk back to the car. As he did so he became aware that the second youth was barring his way; in the heat of the chase he had forgotten all about him. They looked at each other for a moment and then Andrew's head swirled with fury and he took a couple of sudden steps as if to chase the boy who crouched, challenging him like a terrier waiting for a stick. Andrew stopped, half afraid, half aware of the futility of going on with it.

The youth slowly raised two elaborate fingers. "Fuck you," he said, "shitface." He turned and began to jog over to his mate.

Andrew watched him for a moment and slowly turned in defeat. He looked back for the car but it and Lesley had gone.

The aircraft was astonishingly smaller than the Caravelle, the cabin no bigger than a small car. Q noticed with a frisson of alarm that the machine swayed on its undercarriage as he climbed in. When the pilot turned round in his seat with a smile of welcome, Q said, without thinking "It's rather small isn't it? Is this the Cessna?"

"150G," said the pilot. "Very reliable little machine. Not a Comet I'll give you that but it's got a better safety record." He laughed loudly but briefly and moved past Q to close the aircraft's door.

When the engine roared into life the craft vibrated like an ancient loudspeaker, its bumping progress down the sandy strip a considerable contrast with yesterday's velvety take-off. Q had already noticed that the plane had only one engine; he tried not to think about what happened if it failed. As they tumbled into the darkening sky he gripped the sides of his seat as unobtrusively as possible. His legs ached and he realised that his feet were pressed hard against the floor in front of him. Fearful that they might puncture the flimsy fabric of the plane he did his best to relax them and looked nervously out of the window at the garland of lights of the city which yawned sideways away from him.

"Coffee in the flask under your seat," said the pilot after a while. Q nodded. "I'm all right, thanks." He'd forgotten the man's name already. He looked out of the window again. There was a tap on his knee.

"But I wouldn't mind one, thanks." said the pilot.

Q groaned inwardly. He craned stiffly forward, straining to reach the box beneath his feet.

"Probably easier if you undo your belt. You'll never reach it otherwise." The pilot rolled his eyes.

Q hesitated, groping vaguely with the buckle at his waist. He knew really that the belt wasn't holding him in but he could not escape a vision of his body floating helplessly in space. Eventually his fingers found the food-box and he poured the pilot's coffee. His stomach turned and he held the cup out to the pilot as he fought to hold down the surge of bile in his throat.

"Thanks," said the pilot. "Should be there in an hour or so."

Andrew's latest visit to the library had revealed that Koppeh Dagh was a range of mountains on the Iran/Turkmenistan border which would make sense of Rex's last message. 5ZW106 looked like an aircraft registration and he found that the national code for Turkmenistan was in fact KZW; was this a rare but probably unimportant mis-transmission?

At about the time that Q was taking off Peter drank the last of his dark Persian coffee and, helping himself to a last chunk of halva, strolled from the restaurant. Tehran, in the seventies, was a surprisingly dégagé city, given its remoteness from the cosmopolitan West. In those prelapsarian days even at well after midnight the lights burned in restaurants and bars, girls of such elegance and class that they could only be working for the love of it entertained American and French businessmen, putting their prowess and expense accounts under unprecedented strain.

It was still very hot. Peter made his way to the old Citroën Light 11 and, climbing in, started up and drove south down the broad street towards Javadabad and the start of the Dasht-e-Kavir desert.

They were falling at immense speed, the little plane hurtling through the cloud-base. What made it worse for Q was that they weren't even pointing downwards but simply plunging as if in an undersized lift. The air rushed noiselessly from his lungs and he clutched in a fever at the cabin roof, searching for something to hold on to. If only he could black out rather than face the moment, probably only a few seconds away, when they hit the ground and his body would be cracked and broken, crumpled in the stifling cage of the plane.

"Hold on tight," said the pilot. "There might be another one or two of them." He steadied the plane. "We tend to get them over the hills at night. Thermals. What you call air-pockets. The warm air from the ground is sometimes a bit colder over the mountains so the lift's a bit unpredictable. No problem, but you're rather more aware of them in a craft this size."

"Thank you," said Q courteously. "I'll try to remember that."

Peter sat slumped behind the wheel of the Citroën in the dark of the Dasht-e-Kavir desert. He opened his eyes when he heard the Cessna's engine softly break the silence of the night. After a moment he got out. Over to the west he could see the two tiny specks of light at its wingtips.

There was no wind so the pilot could hold his course and land as he was. Peter started the car and flashed his lights three times, on and off. He repeated the procedure twice more and then drove the car in a big circle, parking it so that it pointed away from the plane, its headlights illuminating the stretch of sand in front of him. The plane circled once very low and, dipping like a seagull, swooped low over the car, bounced to a halt and turned back to taxi towards the car. Peter turned off his lights and sauntered over as the engine feathered and died, the propeller stilling itself with a shudder. The pilot got out and walked over to Peter.

"Peter?"

"That's me. Good God, it's you! How are you, Steve, man?"

"Couldn't be better. Piece of cake. Your chummy's a bit ropey though."

"Sick, hey?"

"As a dog."

"I'd better go and say hello."

"Hold your nose, old lad."

Peter approached the plane as Q struggled out, wiping his mouth. A sour smell of vomit drifted from the cabin.

"Good evening, sir," said Peter. "Had a good flight?"

"I've known better," said Q stumbling. Peter put a steadying hand on his shoulder.

"I'm afraid you've come rather a long way for nothing," he said.

George felt better than he had for some time. It had obviously been a purifying experience to get his bitterness off his chest and to discover that he was not alone. He was one of what used to be called the old school, conventional in his approach to life. If a pollster had asked him he would probably have agreed that he was, if vaguely, Christian, had achieved the lower middle class and was broadly conservative. If you poked beneath the surface you would find, to his surprise, a fairly well-developed code of morals. He could not approve of what Peter did – his own tentative work for the Shop he excused on the grounds that he didn't know what was involved – the conscious and calculated switching of sides, the cynically selective release of information, was too coldly clinical to warrant anything but horrified fascination. Yet it had been good for him to hear that some sort of pattern existed, that there was a context into which all his, George's, actions and accidents could be placed.

He felt better about Milena too. Now that he knew that he had been set up he didn't need to be ashamed any more. Curiously he felt no resentment at having been humiliated; it was a kind of relief to him to know that he had been made a fool of rather than having made one of himself.

So he was cheerful and relaxed as he absorbed Milena's instructions about how to handle the boat, how to undertake simple navigation and deal with the various distorted squawks which came from the small radio by the chart table. He felt, he thought, as he watched her move easily around wearing sometimes her tiny scarves, sometimes just a t-shirt, almost brotherly towards her. Everything, it seemed, was under some sort of control and certainly beyond his responsibility. It was going to be a jolly, if energetic, trip. And, for the first time in years, the prospect of exercise was almost appealing.

Q had sat silently in the big Citroën, nursing Peter's hipflask as they watched the Cessna taxi bumpily over the sand, the dust-cloud in its wake glowing fiercely in the yellow glare of the car's headlights. Once it was airborne Peter had switched off the lights and the darkness had mugged them with its blindfold for a few seconds before their eyes struggled to make out the dim shape of the dunes around them and the faint twinkle which might have been the plane or Betelgeuse for all they knew.

Peter had given the whisky a few more minutes to work while Q recovered his spirits and his dignity. Then "If you're ready?" he asked and started the engine.

"How long is the drive?" asked Q as they rejoined the desert road.

"Took me about three hours coming up. We'll be there soon after six. You'll be able to see the sunrise. It's quite a sight."

"I'm sure," said Q.

After a mile or so Q said, "So the SKVP exchange was aborted?"

"Right, sir," said Peter, "that's why we diverted you from Ashkabad back to here. Since they've lost George a second time, their best bet was to keep out of it and pretend it never happened. They were never going to turn up so we were able to save you a bit of a trip."

"But George is safe now?"

"Absolutely. He's on the yacht. Well supervised. And Alex is secure in the embassy."

"How did they get George?"

"Carelessness really. George isn't one of your best-trained agents, sir, now is he? With respect, I think the system of sleepers could do with a little overhaul."

"So it would appear."

After a moment Q asked, "How did you get him back?"

"Good fortune, if I'm honest, at least in Beirut. It's a question of contacts, a matter of who you know. Fortunately I knew the right people on this occasion. Mary's was trickier because it's so remote but we managed to orchestrate a small diversion. Lucky it's mostly an admin place so not seriously defended."

"Why do you think they took him?"

"Because they want to know what the hell he's doing in Beirut. They're deeply suspicious of him. There seems to be no pattern to his activities. All they see are occasional drops of meaningless material, messages in a code so simple a child could break it, which all suggests to them a double code no one has apparently manage to penetrate. Why the hell is he there?"

"Of course. So SKVP hoped that George would tell them?"

"I guess so."

"And did he?"

"Well, if you want my honest opinion, I don't think he's got very much to tell."

Q smiled complacently to himself in the darkness.

"Very perceptive, Peter. Do you think SKVP realised that?"

"So I'm right, am I? He is a stooge. Who can say? I doubt

it, though. They'll probably think George is very ignorant and quite stupid or else a consummate spy. Given the natural paranoia of people in this business I'd say they're more likely to go for the latter."

"That is certainly our intention."

Peter drove on through the wide emptiness.

At length, he turned to Q.

"If George is just a stooge."

"Yes?"

"That suggests that he must be a diversion from some other activity."

"Does it?"

"It's a reasonable assumption."

"But nonetheless only an assumption."

"Okay, but if we accept the assumption for a moment, what could the other activity be?"

"My approach to my job has been to base my actions always on facts, never assumptions. My experience has been that this approach is a sound one. Dealing in hypotheses is a speculative practice. My father, who spent too much of his youth at the casino, told me more than once that all forms of speculation lead with a terrible inevitability to disaster. I have never yet known him proved wrong. Do you know, I believe I can see the beginnings of daybreak. You were right. It's going to be a majestic sight."

"Christ," George thought quietly to himself. "And I'm getting paid for this? Always assuming the bastards are still paying the old retainer into Beirut for me." The thought that they might not did nothing to lessen his warm well-being as he sat among the long early morning shadows on the deck while Milena steered the yacht powerfully through the Saronic Islands. Andrew had spent another useful hour in the library's map section. He had originally put the Cyclades as part of the route but found that they were too far south. And, looking closer at the Times map, he was pleased to discover the Corinth Canal which could cut miles off the journey. It would be perfectly possible for Milena and George to be in Hvar in good time on for the meeting with Q and Peter. Andrew felt a shiver of excitement: they had done this trip for real, whoever they were.

It was a time of day, as George would say, with which he was not familiar. He had had no idea it could be so enchanting. Of course the general atmosphere was greatly enhanced by the sight, if habitual no less entrancing, of Milena wearing practically nothing.

"We cut up past Piraeus and through the Gulf of Patras," she told him. "It save us half a day."

"Whatever you say," murmured George. "But don't hurry on my account."
"No, but we must be in Hvar next week to meet Peter. And Q."

"Ah yes. And Q."

He was pleased that even the thought of Q brought no cloud to his horizon. God, he was in a good mood. He gave way to it contentedly, slumping back in his lounger and watching the sun catch the tiny drift of down at the base of her slender back. No he was in no hurry at all to reach Hvar he thought, feeling excessively fraternal.

SEPTEMBER 3, THURSDAY
LONDON

Tucked into a pocket in the tan leather upholstery of the seat-back, alongside the walnut-faced drinks cupboard, was a rather cumbersome radio telephone. As the car shimmied down Birdcage Walk, the phone warbled. In the front the driver pressed a button releasing the phone into the grasp of an effortlessly elegant hand, on whose little finger a signet ring gleamed dully.

"Rex."

"Message for Q from Peter, Rex. It's not very clear I'm afraid. It says 'George left Mary in a hurry. Hold Alex.' "

"Is that it?"

"Yes, Rex."

"You're right, it's most unclear. We have no idea where George is?"

"None."

"Will you ask Peter to explain urgently what he means?"

"Right away, Rex."

"Thank you."

SEPTEMBER 4, FRIDAY

The Times

Peter in Iran. Sept 3 unclear. Info George's

whereabouts urgent. Rex.

It was late morning when Peter and Q reached the Tehran hotel and they were both in need of sleep. They agreed that they would meet in Q's room at eight o'clock. In the morning they would ostensibly collect Alex from the embassy and take a regular flight to Split; thence by ferry to Hvar. Q went on up while Peter checked them both in. As he was waiting for his key a bundle of newspapers was delivered to the little shop in the foyer. He went over and asked the assistant if the English papers were among them.

She had fine features, a nose slightly too big for European taste, and a dark shadow across her upper lip. She did not smile. "Only Times and Herald Tribune," she said.

"The Times please."

A slight click of the teeth as she came from behind the counter to cut open the bundle. Her body language was unmistakeable; she was doing him a big favour and at some cost to herself. He turned away from her body and its language and picked off the shelf a copy of yesterday's Times. He paid an outrageous price for it and made his way to the lift. As it swished him erratically to his floor Peter unfolded the papers and glanced at the back page. Good, his own message, the bluff about Alex, was safely there. He turned to today's paper and after a moment smiled widely. It was better than he had dared hope. Rex was beginning to be rattled. That mention of Alex had wound him up a notch.

SEPTEMBER 7, MONDAY
HVAR

In the bar of the Adriatic Hotel, now mercifully free of the summer invasion of British tourists, Peter put down his beer and pulled a folded sheet of paper from his shirt pocket. "I thought it might be nice to send Rex a message. Something to put his mind at rest. I've drafted this. I don't know what you think."

Unfolding the paper he pushed it over to Q who read it aloud.

" 'Rex. Entertaining Peter, George and Alex in Pharos Hotel, Hvar. Await instructions. Q.' "

"The Pharos?"

"Don't want to make it too easy for SKVP."

"Of course not. That's very good, Peter, no need to change a thing. Except that George is not actually with us."

"He'll be here in a day or so. I have every faith in his pilot."

Q was almost mellow. He liked the cool wording of the message Peter had drafted for him – very much in the Charles Napier peccavi school of English understatement. Rescuing George, or at least apparently to have been associated with his rescue would do his reputation no harm – not just a desk-man after all, they would mutter approvingly – but, best of all, he had Alex.

The ambassadorial limo had turned up at the Adriatic at 9.30 on Saturday and had taken Peter and Q to the embassy. Half an hour later a man whose head was covered by a blanket had emerged, not wholly unobtrusively, from the rear entrance and been bundled by two other men into the back of the car with them. The car had driven straight onto the section of the runway reserved for diplomatic traffic and the three had headed for the port where they boarded a fast motor-boat and roared away. It had, of course, been a charade for the benefit of any watching stooges, as was the second car which had simultaneously left the front door of the embassy, also with three men, one under a blanket as before and sped off to the airport. Q had seen enough television to do the bit with the hand on the blanket to stop him hitting his head, another nice touch. The three, one still blanketed, had boarded the ambassador's private Heron and a moment later it had taken off, heading north. But it was a charade whose significance was that it proved that the British were taking Alex seriously and whose importance would be confirmed for an observant SKVP when they read the next day's entry in the Times. Alex had been sprung from his cell in Tehran and was now in limbo, a pawn in the hostage game. It was for SKVP to make up its collective mind as to how much of the charade was real and how much mere obfuscation.

SEPTEMBER 9, WEDNESDAY

The Times

Rex. Entertaining Peter, George and Alex in Pharos Hotel, Hvar. Await instructions. Q.

The phone on the ormolu desk by the bed rang only once before the signet-ringed hand put down a Balkan Sobranie and lifted the receiver quietly off its bakelite cradle.

"Yes?"

"Apologies, Rex," came Tenison's courteous voice once more. "Can you talk?"

"I can listen."

"There's been a message from Q. All's well." Tenison found he slipped, probably because he was nervous, into a curiously archaic form of speech when he talked to Rex.

"He, George and Peter are all in Hvar. And Alex."

"Alex?"

"Apparently so. Q would like to know what you want him to do."

"Nothing. I will do anything which needs to be done."

"Yes, Rex."

"Mr Tenison?"

"Yes, Rex."

"Will you take a message? Q's usual channel. It's quite short. Sign it from me."

After a few moments the receiver went down.

"Now, young man," said Rex drowsily. "Where were we?"

SEPTEMBER 10, THURSDAY

The Times.

SKVP. What price Alex now? Rex.

When Q read the mocking entry he was pleased but faintly confused. It was after all SKVP who had raised the issue of Alex as a swap for George. George had been useful to SKVP only as a bargaining chip for Alex whom they clearly wanted back. But what value did Alex have to Rex as a bargain counter? What did SKVP have that Rex wanted to bargain for? Or was it – this suddenly seemed more in character – that Rex simply wanted to rub SKVP's nose in it? Either way Q would have a few days in the sun while they waited for SKVP to respond.

It took Milena and George the best part of five days to motor through Greece and up the coast of Yugoslavia. George, although previously a total stranger to anything smaller than a cross-channel ferry, was now familiar with the size of the craft and, as Milena instructed, he was able to crew it quite satisfactorily. Most of the time, he was glad to find, it was simply a question of setting a course and letting her run. He got almost agile, on their occasional call ashore for provisions, fuel or moorings, at handling the ropes and he compared with increasing envy his rooms in the Beirut Commodore with the effortlessly charming little harbours into which they steered. If even the Commies could make such a good job of a country, he thought, how wonderful it would be if they ever buggered off and left it to the locals to run.

He watched Milena plot their course on the chart table and, as they got closer to Hvar, he became aware of a small knotty tension at the back of his conscious. As he studied it, he realised that he was apprehensive about his meeting with Q. For years now his attitude to his unseen controller had developed from an initially mildly obedient curiosity to the outspoken bolshiness he now felt able to express – or had felt so long as there was no chance that they would ever meet. Now that it was about to happen he realised that he had been wondering what sort of bloke Q would be. He tried to imagine what he looked like and how he would behave. He supposed that he had thought of him as a thin man in a suit, probably with specs, tall, grey-haired. But it was like seeing the film version of a well-liked book. The actor never looked as you imagined the character and afterwards, you could no longer remember your original version. George knew it would be like that with Q – once they had met, his own imagined image would vanish forever.

But what worried him much more was how he, George, would behave towards his superior. His bolshiness and his own clearly-understood idea of his relationship to his masters made him hope that he would react to Q as a colleague, a fellow professional, in a relationship where status didn't really come into question.

On the other hand he could still remember his eighteen months in Catterick twenty-odd years ago. Driving three-tonners for the RASC had done nothing to lessen his dislike of the officer class but he was still reluctantly aware of the curious discipline that National Service had instilled in him. It had, in the end, almost been a relief to succumb to its easy, unchallenged routine and the order which gave each man a certain responsibility, a sense of his own place, even a sort of pride, as if they were all elements of a hugely efficient engine whose power was as unquestioned as it was unobtrusive. How long had it taken George to forget all that? For how many months after demob did he have to control his right hand's urge to snap up a smart one for a passing officer?

He had an uneasy feeling that, in the presence of Q, those twenty years would roll back, that he would conduct himself, not at all as a professional equal but with sturdy deference of a competent NCO up before the colonel.

On the balcony outside his bedroom in the Adriatic Hotel Peter sat talking to a small, sallow, portly man in his sixties with a grizzled crewcut echoed by a bristly moustache. He wore dark shades clipped to his glasses.

"You still haven't said why I should believe anything you say," he was saying. He spoke with a slight French accent. "You have offered me nothing in the way of proof of who you are or why I should listen to your so-called instructions."

"Alex, listen," said Peter urgently. "And please keep your voice down. Can't you see what an opportunity we have? London thinks I'm with them; I've been doubling them for SKVP since 1961. I'm with SKVP. London calls me Peter but my SKVP code is Dima. Check your files."

"What files?" shouted Alex. "Do you think I'm so stupid to carry files?"

"You got caught anyway," Peter couldn't help saying.

Alex glared at him. "I was let down – a failed rv. It happens. You not can depend on people. You will learn this if you spend some time in the field."

"OK, OK. But make a call, hey? Call Pyotr in Tehran. He'll tell you who I am. I'm amazed you don't know already."

"Maybe I never needed to know. And why do you think I should know this Pyotr?"

"Because I know that, in your line, you would have to know him."

"My line! You think you know my line? I worked in embassy that's all. If it suits you British to call me a spy and to invent some, some line for me, what can I do about it?"

"Alex, calm down. I know who you are. I'm not British, I'm South African, I have no interest in being British. I know about your work in the past in Palestine and Persia. I'm on your side."

"There are no sides. Only enemies."

"All right, Alex." Peter sighed and lit a Kool. "But think about it. What have you to lose? The London people don't – I'm sorry – especially value you. They're pleased you fell into their hands, of course, but they don't really need you. But they do value Q. We've got Q out here to look after you. Now we can get Rex if we're clever."

"Rex?"

"Yes, if we use Q as a lure. Supposing we happened to lose Q – perhaps to SKVP – we could get Rex out to handle the hand-back between him and you. Then we simply take Rex and we have everything."

"Why do you want Rex so badly?"

"You're asking the right questions, Alex. Because whatever it is that he and his people are doing, they won't be able to do when we get them. I don't even much care what it is, I just want to stop it."

"Why?"

"Because, if it's British, it's bound to be bad for just about everyone else, except maybe the Yanks. Call it a humanitarian act on behalf of the rest of the globe."

"Interesting idea."

"So, what do you have to lose? If you and I work together we'll both do well by SKVP. But if you try to escape there's a danger that Q will shoot you, and we don't get Rex out. Isn't it worth a gamble that I'm telling the truth, even if you don't call Tehran?"

"Perhaps," said Alex, turning away from the view over the sea to look hard at Peter. "Perhaps I don't need to call Tehran now. But this George fellow, where he fit into all this?"

"That's what we need to find out. Either he's a very smart operator who's giving nothing away or he's a very simple man who genuinely knows nothing and is being used as a pawn. But if it is the latter – and I think it is – what sort of pawn is he? Is he here to cover something up that even he doesn't know about? I think so. But what is it? What is it that they want to distract us from? We have to find out. That's why I'm here. And I think that, not only does Q have the answer but that, whether he wants to or not, he may soon be telling us all about it."

SEPTEMBER 11, FRIDAY
HVAR

The island of Hvar, Andrew read in the guidebook, *has a richly indented coastline which holds many small bays, lapped by warm clear seas. The harbour itself is a perfect example of the Venetian style with elegant warehouses, bars and churches along the waterfront. There is more than adequate mooring for visiting yachts.*

So regular a base was it for sailing even at the time of our story, that new arrivals or departures barely merited the lift of a heavy eyelid for the brown old men who sat, wrinkled, in the shade of the custom house.

Nevertheless when, a little after three in the afternoon, George turned the Stavros Morgana in past the island of Galešnik and into the marina, he rather hoped that by chance Q might be looking out of his hotel window and somehow guess that the quietly authoritative figure at the helm was the agent he had come east to meet after all this time. So confident, if with so little reason, was George now in his seamanship that he handed over the wheel to Milena without demur for her to bring the craft alongside. As she gunned the engine into reverse to bring her to a standstill he jumped almost easily ashore and ran a rope round a bollard before ambling with purposeful expertise to collect the rope which Milena threw him from the cockpit. He almost didn't mind the fumbled catch and the whipped slap of the rope-end across his mouth. He knew what he was doing.

Andrew made a note that he must look up the form as to what happened about immigration, passports and so on when one arrived somewhere in a yacht, especially behind the Iron Curtain. He made another note to try it himself one day; it sounded rather fun.

Ten minutes later, refreshed by his favoured routine of shit, shower and shave, a residue from his army days, George hopped ashore leaving Milena aboard and walked along the harbour towards the Adriatic Hotel.

For his part Q had given no thought to the meeting with George beyond the fact that it had to happen and, although he was indeed sitting on his balcony looking out over the harbour, he had certainly not been watching for George's arrival. George had once again ceased to be important now that his episode was over and the game had moved back to the major players. If he had known about George's own thoughts he would have warned him against the military approach since, although he had nominally spent his war on active service, it had been in a land-based Naval posting as an assistant to a junior equerry at the court of King James. This was thanks to his mother's being the daughter of a Lancashire earl whose estate provided excellent facilities for polo. When war broke out she had barely needed to ask how her son would spend it. The system took charge of everything, even making certain that, thanks to a brief spell with the Intelligence Corps in occupied Germany in the spring of 1945, Q had a D-Day campaign medal to go with the MVO and standard war gongs. It had been fortuitous too in that it found him a peacetime role. Wartime experience in intelligence could, for some, prove to be a valuable passport to a distinctly lucrative career.

The phone by the bed rang and Q ambled in from the balcony. It was Peter.

"He's here," he said. "I said I'd meet him in the bar. Will you join us?"

"Five minutes," said Q.

A quarter of an hour later as George, over his second bottle of Yugoslav chardonnay, was noisily telling a smiling Peter and a silent Alex about his new enthusiasm for sailing, Peter pushed back his chair and stood up, looking over George's shoulder.

"Here's Q," he said.

"Q, this is George," said Peter.

George held out his hand. "Hello, Q," he said. "Good to meet you at last. What can I get you?"

Q allowed George to grasp the ends of his limp fingers. "Thank you," he said without warmth. "I dare say the waiter will deal with that."

Q sat down and, crossing his legs, turned away from George towards the other two. "Enjoying your holiday?"

LIVERPOOL

It was half-past three in the afternoon and the cocktail lounge was empty. They stood at the bar and she leaned forward resting her chin on her hands, watching him carefully while he spoke.

"It's the bluntness I can't take," Andrew was saying.

"You won't believe this now," she said." But in time you will find out that it's true. No matter how empty and depressed you feel now, it's better than not feeling anything at all. Being in love is the best thing in the world but being hurt in love is still better than not being in love at all."

She could not imagine, as she spoke, that he could not need to feel things. She admitted it to herself, she needed passion. When she wasn't in the middle of an affair life seemed a little aimless. And, she knew this was her weakness, she would lose patience with a relationship once it had begun to settle down: those listless goodbyes every morning! She longed for the dagger in the heart, the desperation of knowing that they might never meet again.

She watched Andrew trying to take this in and noticed as he glanced beyond her to the door.

"So there's the guilty couple," said Paula, approaching their table. "I've looked in every pub in town for you two."

Andrew stood awkwardly, out of atavistic courtesy. Paula stood rather too close to him, her hands in her coat pocket.

"Oh dear," said Lesley softly. "I hope you're not going to make a scene."

"Why should I? There's no need is there?" She had a light

Liverpudlian accent.

"This is Paula, as you've probably guessed. And Andrew."

Andrew looked at Paula. She really was very attractive.

"Can I get you a drink?"

"Yes, you can. A pint," she said aggressively. "And don't think you can use your oily charm on me. It won't work."

He went to the far end of the bar where the barman was watching in a disengaged sort of way. The two women were talking fiercely but quietly when he got back. He put the glass down in front of Paula who did not acknowledge it. What should he do? Stand his ground, aim for normality, rely on the British hatred of a row to get them through the next half hour?

"Cheers," he said.

"Oh bollocks," said Paula and he shivered: it was almost sexy. "I've spent hours trying to find Lesley and now that I have I want to talk to her not you, so why don't you just sod off?"

Andrew looked at her. "I think perhaps I will," he said calmly. "Bye then."

"Bye," said Lesley casually, and he walked to the door hoping for but only half-expecting a call to come back. None came, and he went out into the dull splendour of the hotel lobby, shutting the door very gently behind him.

I feel so lonely
Just for you only.

SEVEN

Q had made it plain to Peter that he did not wish to spend the evening in meandering conversation with George. His reasoning, for Peter's purposes, was that it would be difficult for them to avoid shop business and that would be unethical and risky – particularly with Alex on hand. His real reason was that he had nothing to say to George and had no idea what George might want to talk about which could conceivably interest him.

Accordingly, after twenty minutes or so listening to George's account of his recent weeks during which, to his credit, George made no direct or implied comment about his relationship with London, Q stood up.

"You'll have to excuse me," he said. "As Peter knows I've one or two things to do. You'll look after Alex, won't you, Peter? We'll meet tomorrow."

"Do you know?" said George after he'd gone. "He's almost more of a fartarse than I thought he would be. I had him down as a tall, thin, specs, arrogant public school bastard. In fact he's a small, tubby, no specs arrogant public-school bastard. Oh well. Three out of six isn't bad."

"I expect he improves on acquaintance," said Peter with a smile. Alex snorted.

"Give him time, Alex," said Peter. "He takes a little getting to know, I expect."

"I have no time to give him," said Alex coldly.

"We shall have to be generous with our time with Q," said

Peter. "There's a lot he has to tell us."

"I find gun at side of head loosen the tongue very effectively," retorted Alex.

"Well let's hope it doesn't come to that."

Later Peter walked with Alex and George back to the harbour. Peter had suggested to Q that the yacht was a more secure place to keep Alex confined than the hotel. Milena greeted Peter with controlled delight, George with a warm wink and, George noticed, Alex with cool politeness. He assumed she'd met him before and did not care for him.

Later still as he lay on his bunk, the narrowness of which he could still not quite get used to, he heard Peter's low voice, indecipherable through the bulkhead, and Milena's gurgling chuckle. "Nice people" thought George. "They deserve each other".

SEPTEMBER 12, SATURDAY

"I know you don't like talking of hypotheses," said Peter, "but when do you think we might hear from SKVP?"

He and Q were sitting in the bow of the Stavros Morgana which now rocked almost imperceptibly at her mooring in the harbour. Peter had moved her from her spot in the marina, alongside the other yachts, jammed together like hard silvery sardines, to a floating anchor-buoy a hundred yards away. A light offshore breeze stirred a strand or two of Peter's hair. There was no chance of their conversation being overheard.

"You're right, I don't, and I don't know. As I say I find to easier to deal with situations where I know the facts rather than trying to speculate."

"But you must surely have to keep one or two options open? Two anyway: a course of action if they don't get back to us and another if they do."

"If they don't respond – which seems unlikely given that we have Alex – we shall go home. If they do, our response will depend on what they say."

"And if you go home, what else happens?"

"What else?"

"To Alex, to me, to George."

"Alex will come with me to London where he will be detained at Heathrow as an illegal immigrant until the Home Office are instructed to sort him out. You and George will carry on as before."

There was a silence.

"I know it's the very essence of your business to be discreet," said Peter eventually.

Q smirked inwardly.

"And I know that you wouldn't want to tell me anything in detail but it would be very helpful to me in our future relations if you could, how shall I say, put me in the picture about George's end of the operation."

"Why is that?"

"Because it is, as you must know from your own experience in the field, very hard to make decisions when you don't know as much as is possible about the elements of the game."

"But, Peter, you do know as much as is possible. I'm tempted to say that, as an agent in the field, your job is not to take decisions but to act upon the decisions made by others."

"Like you."

"Exactly so."

Peter smiled broadly.

"Well I'm tempted to say that you have been out of the field for too long. But I don't want to argue the point. In any case I'm sure that you want to talk to Alex this morning."

"That was my plan."

"I'll fetch him for you. I'm sorry to have asked a difficult question."

"Not a problem. Think no more of it."

"Oh, I think I just might," said Peter to himself as he moved aft.

George, who was sitting curiously neatly for a man of his bulk, in a canvas chair, opened an eye as Peter passed him. Neither spoke. A moment later Peter returned with Alex and escorted him forward to where Q sat. George heard the murmur of their voices and then saw Peter retreat and sit on the deck a couple of discreet yards away, his back against the forward cabin wall. George noticed with only a momentary lurch of his stomach that Peter held a small revolver in the hollow of his large hands. It was a measure of George's progress into the amoral world of intelligence that after a moment's thought, he shrugged his shoulders, aware that there was nothing he could do. He dozed sporadically.

He dreamed absurdly that he was waiting for a train in the main station of some European city – he didn't recognise it. When he reached the platform he had to climb several steps to find a seat and, turning back towards the track, realised that he was in some sort of stadium; another huge bank of seats on the other side of the track was filled with people waiting more or less motionlessly. A young woman walked along the front edge of the platform looking up to the crowd. "I'm looking for a volunteer," she cried with great enthusiasm and a confident smile. George had the absolute certainty that she was going to choose him but was spared the consummation of his fear by the sound of Peter's approaching feet scuffing lightly on the deck in front of him. Alex was nowhere to be seen.

"Haven't lost him, old cock?" said George, less coherently than he would have wished.

"No, no, back in his cabin, safe and sound," said Peter with a wink. So that's where Milena got it.

Peter sauntered on by and sat down with Q again.

"How did you get on?" he asked.

"I've known better," said Q. "But it's only the start and the first stages are always tricky. You need time to get to know each other and let a relationship form."

"A relationship? Isn't it a rather one-sided one?"

"Not at all, it's a very intriguing balance, very symmetrical. The questioner has a desire for a certain amount of knowledge, although he doesn't know the details. The other has a good deal of knowledge which he has been trained to keep absolutely secret. And what is your basic instinct when someone tells you a secret? To share it with someone. And the more vital the information, the more imperative it is to keep it from your interrogator, the more powerfully seductive the urge to spill nuances and resonances. Both sides know this, both sides, almost like two lovers, know how it will end but will it be tonight, tomorrow, next week? There's a complicity in interrogation undreamed of by those who haven't experienced it."

"So the person in the chair really wants to let his information go?"

"It's half the reason for his having become an agent in the first place; it's a sort of challenge to himself to see how long he can last. But the release is exquisite."

"You mean they feel better for having talked? I can't believe that."

"Only to start with. It's still like sex, particularly of the solitary kind. There is this wonderful, draining climax, the logical end of everything that's happened to him, the end of physical pain, the purification of no longer holding a secret; this is followed, disappointingly fast, by the anti-climax, the sense of waste, emptiness, failure and despair. This is the time when you need to be certain that the cyanide capsules have been safely removed. There are more cases of people committing suicide after having talked than beforehand."

"But you haven't reached that stage with Alex?"

"Lord no, still some way to go. But I have a hunch that there is mutual self-interest in this on a larger scale. I think it suits SKVP not to make a fuss about our arrest of Alex because they don't want us to know they're rattled. And if they don't want us to know they're rattled, they probably are. Which means that Alex is probably up to something quite spectacularly sinister somewhere. But where? Surely not in Tehran itself. He wouldn't bother himself with the poor old Shah's rickety secret service which, in any case, is doing a perfectly reasonable job of keeping down the dissidents. Can't see any threat to the old man from inside and I can't believe any of the Arab states want to dirty their hands in there. So the question we need Alex to answer is where his centre of operations is; once we know that we can probably deduce the nature of the business itself. And, as it happens, I think it quite suits us to keep this low key precisely because we can't lay any specific charges. Being caught helping yourself to a bundle of top-secret files isn't a very convincing charge when the files vary from the CIA's post-Mossadeq shenanigans to speculations on the possibility of a freeze on oil exports. Nothing very incriminating there."

"But he will tell you in the end?"

"They always do. Not always everything but enough."

"And what about the information about George? Will you give that away?"

"Hardly the same thing. But the answer's no, one because it's not important enough to me and, two, because it's not important enough to anyone else."

"How do you know that?"

"Because, apart from your routine enquiries earlier, I have absolutely no evidence that anyone is interested in George."

"Does that negate his value?"

"Not at all. At least not necessarily. If I said more, that would, in itself give away something about George's function."

"Precisely."

"I'm sorry?"

"I said 'precisely'. That's precisely why I'm asking."

"About George?"

"Yes. I want to know about George. There's your evidence

that someone is interested."

"No but, Peter, this is a purely academic interest. It's part of your understandable desire to know as much about everything as you can. It's not the same."

"Q, how can I convince you that I'm serious? I suppose in all these relationships between interrogator and interrogated, the key is the balance of power. The one with more power at the end is the one who wins."

"As you say."

"But the odds are tilted in favour of the interrogator because he makes all the running. He chooses when the interview starts and stops for instance."

"Well actually not always but, in general, yes you're right."

"And most of all he has an advantage because the prisoner knows that, whatever he says, he may be shot at any time."

"That certainly offers an advantage to the home side."

"So, to mix a metaphor, the existence of a gun loads the dice."

"The idea of a gun is just as effective."

"So, if I said, and I'm trying to avoid all melodrama here, if I said that I had a gun in my pocket, here, now, would the idea of a gun be enough to convince you that I was serious?"

For the first time, and quite suddenly, Q became aware that this was not, in fact, a purely hypothetical debate. He was not used to being surprised. For a moment his head swam.

"That would depend," he said carefully, "on whether or not I was convinced that the gun was real – and the intention to use it."

"It's quite real," said Peter. "Want to see it?" He tugged the little pistol from his pocket – hard to do when you're sitting down. "9 mm Makarov if you're interested."

"So it is."

"And now?"

"Well now my approach depends, as I say, on how likely I think you are to use it."

"Have no doubts, Q," said Peter evenly. "I want the information and I will kill to get it."

"I must learn to be less trusting." said Q. "I should have realised that someone like you wouldn't want to be committed to one organisation, let alone one set of principles. Loyalty is such hard work and so boring. Anyway, sorry to sound like one of those films but, if you kill me, you won't get the information."

"That's something you're going to have to think about, hey Q?" replied Peter, his polite English giving way for a moment to a Boer snarl. "Here's the gun; here am I; and here's the question one more time. What exactly is George up to hey? I'm going to give you an hour – I know you won't try to get away – and then I shall ask you the question again. And I hope that our relationship will allow you to reply."

"So that's what Alex meant. 'Know your enemy.' I suppose he meant you."

"I'm not your enemy, Q. We work together, we have much in common. All I want is for us to be comrades and for you to share with me some of the facts which govern our collaboration." He pressed the muzzle of the gun briefly to the side of Q's head. "I'll see you in an hour."

George did not hear as Peter scuffed past him; the booze and the sun had done well. Peter went below, knocked on the door of Alex's cabin and went in.

"It will be interesting to see if he talks," said Peter.

"You think he will?"

"I have a nasty suspicion that he won't. Somewhere inside him is the sense that British people don't do that sort of thing even if they want to because it's bad form; it's letting the side down. Even if what they tell us is completely harmless."

"And if he doesn't?"

"I'll have to shoot him."

"Why?"

"Because if I don't I will lose all credibility. Having told him that I'll kill him if he doesn't give me the information, I can hardly not do it. In any case I've blown cover now; he knows he's made a mistake about me and he'd have me taken out within a month."

"But does he know where find you? You're plenty experienced in field, you have plenty cover."

"But I should be distracted by the knowledge that he had someone looking for me which might, just by accident perhaps, stumble across me. I couldn't operate like that. Anyway why are you so worried? Don't you want me to shoot him?"

"I never like cold blood killing. Life is not, you could say, worth it."

"A pacifist spy. What a curious idea."

"Not perhaps pacifist but certainly peace-loving."

"So you think I shouldn't shoot him?"

"I do. But not my problem. Your problem."

"Well can you give me a reason why I shouldn't?"

"No, Peter, I can't give and I won't give. If you want kill him, then do. If not, don't. But please don't try wrap me up in what you decide and – please – don't ask me find you excuses not to do it."

"Well thanks for the lecture, hey." Peter bent his head with a thin smile. "Nice to have a moralist aboard."

He went out and closed the door quietly behind him.

Alone, sitting facing out over the steel blue of the harbour, Q tried to remember the tips his training had given him on how to deal with such a situation. He realised with a grim interior smile that he had subconsciously regarded this part of his training as somehow irrelevant. He had known, with an embarrassment which he kept to himself, that he was never likely to be exposed in the field, that his background, breeding and connections had established him before day one as a potential controller, administrative rather than executive. He had been intrigued in an academic kind of way to hear the stories the senior instructors had told of the life and death fixes in which they had found themselves and in which they, the trainees, would certainly one day experience for themselves. He had admired the quiet and restrained way in which the trainers had described their escapes, had been impressed with the subtle and skilful ploys which might help him to escape in his turn. But he had not kept hold of it in his mind as he might a real lesson; it had the impact of fiction rather than fact, briefly stimulating but ultimately of no lasting value.

So he had never learned, not really learned, how to survive

under torture, nor how to give away information which might convincingly satisfy an enemy without compromising his own masters. He simply could not remember the drill. But, more curiously, as he recalled the hard pressure on his temple, he found that he could not really concentrate. He could not take seriously even now the thought that Peter really meant to kill him, and the stunning fact of Peter's duplicity was not even of passing interest. He knew dully that he was probably going to die but, instead of trying to find ways to survive: escape, surrender, whatever it might take, he could think only of his family. It was only days since he had left the house in Haslemere, told Jean he'd be back in a day or two and, feeling rather proud and adventurous, hugged his teenage son and daughter. He was, to his colleagues, an aloof, even cold man but they would have been surprised to know how relaxed he was with his family and how happy they seemed to be with him. Even the coldest most humourless official, they would have realised, can fall in love, inspire passion and desire in others, and laugh, play and talk in silly voices. If some of Q's colleagues had thought back to their own schooldays they would have remembered the same syndrome at work with their teachers: crazed eccentrics in term-time, with baggy jackets and stained trousers who rode wobbly bicycles, they could sometimes be seen during the holidays dancing rather well with their wives and driving fast cars with practised aplomb. Q was one of these and it was perhaps his tragedy and even his comfort that, even at the apparent end of his life, he could not think of how to save it but only of how much he had enjoyed the love of his family and, helplessly, how he would miss them.

And, when you leave me
I know you'll grieve me…

The business of getting over the loss, death or departure of someone you love has, Andrew realised, dangerously negative implications.

There is such a strong, often unconscious desire to remember the good times that one picks constantly at the scab, never allowing forgetfulness to heal it over. Add to this the inevitable and frequent accidental associations of people, opinions, places and events with happier times, – "there are so many cafés and pubs I can't visit now because you and I went there together", an ex-girl friend had told Andrew when they had bumped into each other months after the break-up – and normal life can become impossibly difficult if one is forever choking on a lump of nostalgia.

It is aggravated still further in broken liaisons, by jealousy of a third person. Instead of accepting his or her presence and one's replacement by them, there is an unhealthy urge to know where they are and what they are doing; to confirm to oneself one's worst fears about the seriousness of the new relationship.

Lesley had been right, Andrew thought. Better to make the cut, dress the wound and occupy the mind with the alternative present and future while the wound heals. He was, he realised, coming to believe that there might come a time when there wasn't even a scar to show for it. Hatred, by building up his self-esteem, had become an effective analgesic; already the pain had become more focused, more manageable. He had already begun to hate her and it was this scorn which, if he was lucky, would sustain him over the years, which would protect him, keep him sane and preserve his self-respect until, at last, the day would come, long after it had ceased to matter, when he realised that he had completely forgotten her.

George woke with a start to find Peter squatting beside him.

"Good God, Peter! How long have you been there?"

"Only a moment or so. I'm on my way to talk to Q again."

"Oh, ah yes, of course," said George vaguely. "Making any progress?"

"Not so far, I'm afraid. He's not a very talkative fellow."

"Rather how he struck me, I must say." He paused. "Um, has he, you know, have you explained the position to him?"

"Yes, I have. Quite simply, but he took my meaning, I guess."

"But, er, no real response yet?"

"No, I gave him an hour to think things over."

"How long ago was that?"

"About an hour."

"And now what happens?"

"I shall ask him again for the information I need."

"And, if he doesn't tell you?"

"I shall shoot him."

"Good God. Right. Sorry, all this kind of thing's a bit of a new one on me. I mean I know it's always part of the plot but I've never actually come across it before."

"Don't you want me to shoot him?"

"No! Christ, Peter, I don't know. I mean it's nothing to do with me. I've got nothing personal against the bloke but I'm not in your league. It's not the kind of decision I get called on to make. You know I'm not the sort of bloke they give guns to."

"So you're happy that I do it?"

"No! Look, old mate. That's like asking me if there's mercury on the moon. I'm not equipped to answer. Personally, as I say, it's not my line. I couldn't conceivably do that sort of thing and I'd much rather no-one else did either. But what do I know about anything? I couldn't kill someone in a thousand years."

He stared at Peter in anguish. "I thought you once said something about valuing human life." he said.

"Yes. And I also said that you sometimes have to get rid of people who get in the way of progress."

Peter walked away and, once again, sat down facing Q. George screwed up his eyes and gripped the arms of his chair trying to block his ears by will power. He remembered going to a performance of Toad of Toad Hall when he was about ten. There had been a moment when Toad, Mole, Rat and Badger had appeared in front of the curtain during a scene change, en route for the battle of Toad Hall. Toad carried a huge old-fashioned flintlock which he brandished elaborately around him. George had known that, at some stage, it was going to go off and that there would be a terrible bang and he would jump nearly out of his skin. He realised that the waiting was going to be quite as bad as the bang itself and he hardly heard a word of the scene, so fixed was his attention on the great gun. Needless to say, when it did go off, he leapt in his seat and his heart pounded with shock. The knowing had not prepared him at all. And now, as he watched, he found that he was trembling with fear and anticipation. He knew that something was going to happen, something monstrous, beyond his control, something which he had never thought to see. If only, he thought, he hadn't known what Peter would do. He had to watch, how could he look away at anything else when that was happening a few yards away? He knew too, with the absolute certainty of the gambler, that nothing would stop it. Q would not talk, Peter would not spare him. Their roles were cast.

He braced himself to try to stop the panic-tremble which shook his whole body and to prepare himself for the moment. He heard, almost with relief, Q raise his voice saying something like "You know I bloody well can't!" and he watched as Peter glanced quickly to left and right over the bows of the yacht and leaned forward very close to Peter as if to embrace him. He said something to him, almost in his ear, there was a small thump from somewhere and Q shuddered slightly and sat back in his chair.

Peter sat for a few moments then stood up slowly and, without looking back at Q, walked towards George unscrewing the silencer.

"Is that it?" asked George softly.

"That's it."

"Oh, Christ. Are you just going to leave him there?"

"For the moment. He won't attract attention there. When it's dark we'll tidy him away."

George's mouth was foully dry.

"What did you say to him? At the end?"

"I said 'Goodbye'."

The Times

Rex. Uninvited guest night 11/12. Q missing.

Moving to Blue 2. Peter.

SEPTEMBER 14, MONDAY
LONDON

Mondays were usually good days for Tenison. Fridays, on the other hand were frequently a disappointment. They held the promise of the imminent weekend and he always hoped that would simply fulfil that hope and slide easily into a leisurely two days at home. They seldom did. Often they started tantalisingly well: the sun shone, people returned his calls, he tidied up some of those dreary bits of postponed business, the desk began to clear a little and he could even hope to start the new week with a fairly clean slate. But too often, towards five o'clock, just as he might be thinking of a getaway his phone would ring and it would be some superior who had just remembered a job that absolutely must be done before Saturday, or an inferior who, having been battling all day with a self-inflicted cock-up, finally lost his nerve and with guilty relief, referred upwards to Tenison and went home. Mondays, by contrast, were mostly days where he could start the day with a cleanish sheet, make some plans, map things out before the phone started to ring.

This Monday was exceptional in so far as his phone rang that morning even before he had taken his coat off. He answered with what he hoped was cool weariness.

"I have Rex for you," said his secretary whom he imagined clapping her hand over her mouth, stifling a wide-eyed giggle at her colleague. The girls knew instinctively how he feared Rex and were pleased with the power it gave them to cut him down.

"Good morning, Rex."

"Just one moment, Mr Tenison," came the voice of Rex's secretary. "I'll put Rex through."

Tenison rolled his eyes. He hated these power games the secretaries played, scoring points off each other if they made the other wait for their boss to come on the line. The line clicked.

"Yes?" said Rex.

"Good morning, Rex," said Tenison again.

"I take it you've seen the paper?"

Tenison's heart sank. He had read the Telegraph, which he preferred, on the Tube. Thinking that SKVP would take some time to reply, he had planned to scan the Times in the office later. Clearly there had been something in the column and now Rex wanted his reaction.

"Hasn't come up yet, maddeningly," he said rapidly. "I take it there's a message?"

There was a pause which, Tenison felt, had an edge of exasperation.

"It appears that Q is missing."

"My God."

"It's a problem." The voice was quiet, feline. "It must be odds on that SKVP have got him somehow. They will almost certainly use him to make a demand within a few days. He will be useless to them, of course, except as a hostage."

"Of course."

"What do you think they will want?"

"An exchange with Alex?"

"I think so. What would you advise?"

"On balance, Rex, I'd be tempted to let them have him. As we know, Alex isn't much good to us but Q is vital. It would be a bit of a blow to our pride and SKVP would certainly reckon to have won a points victory, but it doesn't leave us materially worse off than we were before we got Alex."

Tenison could hear Rex's soft breathing in his ear.

"I think you're right, Mr Tenison," said Rex after a moment. "How shall we effect the exchange?"

"It depends where Peter is, I think, Rex."

"He's moving to Blue 2. Where's that?"

"Western Adriatic; he could be anywhere between Bari and Rimini. It would put him out of immediate danger if SKVP are still around but would give him time to rush back if we discover where Q is."

"We should respond positively to SKVP when they send word what they want. At the same time we should put out an ambiguous message to Peter. We must make SKVP think that we're still making the running. And we trust that Peter will pick up any signals from SKVP about the exchange arrangements?"

"He's very reliable."

"He's managed to lose Q."

Tenison was silent. There was nothing to say.

"But you trust him?"

"I don't think we have any option, Rex."

"Well we had better read the paper tomorrow."

The telephone went down at the other end.

Damn. Another Monday cocked up. SKVP's message might come tomorrow in which case he would have to make the necessary arrangements. Meanwhile he could work on what he might say if they did in fact demand a swap with Alex. He was unhappy about the whole business and particularly about Peter. Rex was right. How could they rely on him if he'd managed to lose Q?

Lose Q? It was unimaginable. He could only assume that Q had pulled rank and gone for a walk or something to demonstrate his independent spirit and had gone a block too far. If that was the case it was a pretty elementary mistake. What could Q have been thinking of? He must have enough experience to know not to expose himself like that. In a way it was chance that he'd been picked up, or at least handed over to, SKVP given the number of rogue petty mafiosi who made a reasonable living by rolling Westerners. Q was not the sort of Englishman who could effortlessly blend into the camouflage of a foreign country. Whatever he wore, he would always be as conspicuous as if he were dressed in a stripy blazer and a boater on his head. Pity they hadn't just got Alex; it would have been a loss of face but would have caused far less trouble. It was annoying that, Alex having seemed intriguing enough for Q to go out, it now seemed to confirm that he was indeed a major player, bigger than they'd thought, if they wanted him back that badly.

Tenison stared uneasily out of his window. Something didn't fit. He buzzed his secretary and asked her to bring him in a copy of today's Times.

"It's just come up, sir," she said, and a moment later she brought it in.

He looked down the personal column. Oh hell. There it was:

> **Rex. Uninvited guest night 11/12. Q missing.**
>
> **Moving to Blue 2.**

Well, of course, he'd been jumping to conclusions. He had for a moment allowed himself to assume that Rex's hypothesis was already fact. They hadn't yet said they wanted Alex. That was reassuring, wasn't it? On the other hand it was clear that they couldn't have just stumbled on Q. According to Peter, there had been some sort of raid on the yacht during which Q had been snatched. That suggested they knew exactly what they were after. It also seemed to suggest that, after all, perhaps Alex wasn't so important since, if they could grab Q, they could probably have taken Alex as well. And Alex would have gone willingly. Willingly? For Christ's sake, Alex was part of SKVP wasn't he? Why would they deliberately leave him behind? No, hang on a minute, we don't know that they have left him behind. Except that Peter would surely have mentioned it if he'd been taken too. Perhaps Peter had managed to disturb them before they could get Alex. After

all, presumably Alex was locked up somewhere while Q
might just have been strolling on deck. Even so. Just
suppose they really didn't want Alex and that he was just a
decoy? What would they want in exchange for Q? Nothing
material surely? No planes to Beirut, or money or guns;
they had plenty of arms and entirely free access across the
world, especially the Middle East which the USSR so
lavishly supplied with goods and materials. What was so
important to them that they would consider trading Q for?
If it wasn't goods it had to be a person. Who did they
know about in the organisation? His skin suddenly chilled.
Christ, they couldn't..?

He buzzed his secretary. "Would you try Rex for me?"

His phone rang seconds later and he felt suddenly
doubtful; he hadn't expected Rex to be there.

"Yes?" came the breathy voice.

"Sorry to trouble you, Rex," he said clumsily. "I've just
been doing some thinking about the SKVP business."

"Oh good," said Rex with not quite enough genuine
warmth.

"I know that the prime reason for an exchange must
obviously be Alex."

"I think so."

"But it just occurred to me that, if they don't want Alex –
and, if they do, why didn't they take him with Q? – there's
just a chance that they might – I mean the only other
person they know about – who's gone public as it were –
is, um, you."

Tenison was treated to one of Rex's elegant pauses.

"Mr Tenison, I'm almost flattered. Is that said after due

reflection?"

"Yes, Rex. Well it is a bit off the top of the head I admit but I think it's a serious possibility and, if I may say so, you mustn't fall for it."

"Mustn't I?" Tenison could imagine the patronising smile. "Are you saying that you would consider swapping me for Q?"

"Of course not, Rex. But someone here might think it worth your going out to bait a trap. To spring Q. I think that would be very very unwise. For, um, for obvious reasons."

"That's nice to know. Well let's hope it doesn't come to that."

The phone went down again and Tenison wished he'd thought longer before calling Rex. He was making an idiot of himself.

By the time George had woken from what he realised guiltily had been a long and peaceful sleep life on board the boat was already astir. Emerging from his cabin with what, he also realised, was a now-habitually clear head, George saw Milena and Peter leaning over the chart-table. Peter heard George's shuffling arrival and waved him over.

"Good morning," he said. "Milena's been for the papers. Still too early for today's but I like the look of yesterday's very much."

He put his finger on the front page of the Times he had opened on the table. George bent closer to read the entry. He straightened. "You must have put this in a couple of days ago," he said. " 'Q missing' So you always intended to kill him whatever happened," he said. It was not a question.

"I've known Q for a long time and people like him," said Peter evenly. "Certainly long enough to be able to form an opinion as to when and if they tell you what you want to know. But, as I told you yesterday, I had to blow my cover with Q and, once I'd done that he was, well, redundant I suppose. We had gone as far as we could together and he would have done to me later what I had to do sooner to him."

"And where's Blue 2?"

"You're going to like it. Gulf of Venice."

"What for?"

"Easier access to neutral territory, easier to hide. Better comms. And easier for Rex to get to."

"You think you've got a chance of getting him to come out?"

"Oh, I'm sure he'll come. We've made him an offer, as they say in Sicily, he can't refuse. If we had today's paper I could show you. Milena do we have the text?"

Milena opened a drawer above the chart table and drew out a slip of paper. Peter handed it to George.

Rex. Q for Alex? Confirm within 3 days. SKVP.

George found that he couldn't bear to look at Peter. The cold-bloodedness of it all chilled him.

"Still playing the double identity then?"

"No choice, man. I have to get Rex out here. It's the only

way to find out what London's game is."

"It's that important?"

Peter banged his fist on the table suddenly.

"Oh, for Christ's sake, George, don't play so bloody innocent with me. You know what the stakes are. You know the game: you play it too even if in a rather junior league. It's my job to find out about London. My life depends on it. That's how it is in this game. Q knew that. Rex knows too, which is why he'll come. And just before you start getting too self-righteous about it, you might think about where you come into all this and how much of a factor your own life is. How much do think it counts for? Have you any idea? No. If you were any cleverer than I think you are, you'd probably be down there with Q. It's only because I take you at face value and reckon that you really don't have any bloody clue what you're really involved in that there's no point. Lucky for you you're no threat to anyone so far as I can see. But you might just get to be a nuisance and frankly man, nuisances are pretty expendable. So my advice to you is keep schtum, keep out of my way and don't do too much thinking hey? I'm running this show and I intend to do it right. And you better pray that I do because that's your best chance to stay alive."

Once again his voice had taken on the aggressive fricatives and pointed vowels of the native Afrikaaner: arrogant, contemptuous and utterly self-possessed. Milena stood quite still through this, looking hard at the charts. As he tried to make a dignified departure George caught her eye. It did not wink.

George climbed the steps out of the chart-room and into the cockpit. He was amazed at how angry he was.

Throughout his easygoing life he had had people shout at him; he was one of those people at whom people shout. He absorbed it or it ran off his back or somewhere; it seldom affected him. He had always had the enviable ability not to take personally criticisms which were accurately and cruelly personal. Irritatingly for his antagonist, he hardly seemed to hear them. But just now the skin seemed suddenly thinner. Not that he had bothered much with the detail of what Peter had said but the simple fact of being shouted at by a man with whom he had less and less sympathy had wormed its way under that hitherto impervious hide. For almost the first time in his life he thought of answering back. He stopped abruptly and turned. Leaning with some elegance he thought on the frame of the hatch he asked casually:

"Where did you say Q was? Down there I think you said. Down where exactly?"

Peter smiled, his anger gone, amused at George's plucky stand. "As they say, perhaps also in Sicily, he eats with the fishes."

George was pleased that he kept his face impassive.

"And Alex?"

"Alex is also below but not so far. He's in his cabin, waiting."

"For?"

"For Rex to bite. We have three days, rather more in fact, allowing Rex time to fly out. Time to enjoy a relaxed cruise up to Venice or Chioggia perhaps. Venice, on balance."

What is shocking about death is that so often the brain is working right up until the final moment when the body finally packs up. George was trying to understand what he felt about Q's murder and to get to grips with the finality of that nanosecond which separates a sentient, breathing, talking man from a corpse, that infinitesimal bridge between living and being dead. At one moment there is a thinking, arguing man, a creation with a brain of amazing sophistication, with countless thoughts, feelings, attitudes, opinions, affections, fears, and in a moment all this is extinguished. There remains nothing but a huddle of clothed flesh incapable of reacting to the heaviest of blows or the most vigorous resuscitation. This man with all his history, his hinterland, his parentage, his schooling, his colleagues, his books, his enemies, was now nothing, could feel nothing, say nothing, hear nothing, inspire nothing. George wondered whether killers ever wanted to revive their victims. Perhaps they hadn't quite realised themselves the finality of death. In life you usually got a chance to correct mistakes – but just not where death was concerned.

He knew that Q was dead, it wasn't that he couldn't believe it; simply he found it fascinating. It had almost been a privilege to witness that ultimate change of state.

Some years earlier a friend of his had been seriously ill. George had gone to see him regularly in hospital and they had chatted as if they had both been in the pub. The conversation was heightened by the fact that they both knew that it could be their last. And yet the idea of death seemed remote and as unreal as ever, at least to George, despite the drip and the medical apparatus. George wondered whether his friend felt the nearness of mortality and whether he wanted to talk about it. If he did he wasn't letting on, perhaps, George guessed, because to admit it might somehow appear to accept it.

When George went to the hospital one morning to be told that his friend had died during the night, he felt cheated. Suddenly his friend was inaccessible to him, no longer there to talk and be talked to. Not there to say goodbye to, as George now wished he had been able to do. The protocol of death and burial had taken him over; he had seen the last of him.

And yet it still seemed unreal. How could anyone so obviously alive, even if weak and ill, be dead? It was easier to imagine that he had gone abroad indefinitely, miles away but alive, than to accept the reality of his dead presence. Even though he had seen him, unconscious for a time, wired up to the machinery, ghastly and stertorous, it was impossible to accept that he was now just a cadaver. No amount of preparation, of trying to imagine what was going to happen; nothing had warned him of the implacable finality of his friend's going. He understood why families need to see their relative's lifeless corpse, to understand the deadness of the body and the utter final absence of the personality.

And it was the same with Q. He hadn't known him but he had had an existence. George had seen him breathe and talk and move. Even watching him die had made it no easier to accept.

In the late afternoon, after the fiercest heat of the sun had been absorbed by the hilltop villas of the town and a light breeze skiffed over the harbour, Peter unhitched the *Stavros Morgana* from the mooring buoy and headed her west towards the harbour mouth and open sea. A yellow buoy bobbed on the iridescent slick of the harbour. Its paint was flaking and the anchor chain, a green and black belt of slippery steel links, was badly fouled with weed and barnacles. In the winter or perhaps next year the marina authorities would send a team of labourers to repair the buoys and clean up their chains and anchors before the spring influx of tourist yachts. It was not a job they cared for but it paid. The anchor, embedded deep in the sea bottom, always required a big effort to heave up. Next time it would seem to need even more than before, as if it had snagged on something. The young men in their sturdy rowing boat would mutter under their breath as they strained at the chain, and their grumbling would turn first to puzzlement, then to a cold fear as, when the anchor finally toppled over the gunwale into the slopping water in the bottom of the boat, it brought with it a large and slimy tarpaulin bag from whose rotted fabric oozed a puddle of greenish decaying flesh at which a few tenacious fish still dartingly nibbled.

EIGHT

SEPTEMBER 15, TUESDAY
LONDON

Tenison had got up early and bought a paper from the newsagent rather than wait for the office delivery. He scanned the column rapidly. There it was.

> Rex. Q for Alex? Confirm within 3 days. SKVP.

Well it was a relief in some ways. Alex was what they wanted, rather than Rex. But it was a bugger that, unless they could finesse SKVP on the exchange, they would never know how important Alex really was.

The phone was ringing as he opened his office door.

"Have you seen today's paper?"

It was Rex, who didn't bother with introductions when he bypassed his secretary.

"Yes, I have."

"I thought you might be reassured that they don't seem to want me after all."

There seemed to be some distortion on the line, a sort of regular vibration. Tenison tensed. Was there some sort of device on the line?

"That's good news, Rex," he said formally. "Um, is this line quite secure? I can hear a kind of buzzing."

"Buzzing?" said Rex and laughed, something Tenison had never heard before. It was a curiously husky laugh, almost sensual but wholly without warmth.

"Don't worry, Mr Tenison. That's Buster. He's purring because he's just going to have breakfast. By the way, Mr Tenison, I have decided to take your advice. We are going to accept SKVP's offer of an exchange of Q for Alex. Perhaps you could see to it that through the usual channels."

"Right away, Rex."

And, just so that we can check how much Peter is on his mettle, let's see whether he can deduce what he has to do from our message to SKVP. We'll send him a little reminder in a day or so. All right?"

"Absolutely."

"Good."

SEPTEMBER 18, FRIDAY

The Times

SKVP. Affirmative. My yacht still in your area.

Available for meeting. Rex.

SEPTEMBER 19, SATURDAY

The Times

Peter in Adriatic. Maintain silence. Be ready to sail at half hour's notice. Rex.

SEPTEMBER 20, SUNDAY

Peter punched two triangular holes in another can of cold beer. He was happy. The sailing had been good, they had made Rimini in three days and he had had no difficulty in finding a newsagent which could provide him with yesterday's Times – recently delivered – but also the day before's. The news looked good. Rex was making the right noises and, in particular, the second message with its suggestion of the need for emergency action, hinted that Rex really might have taken the bait.

Of course, he realised, it was a clever piece of work by Rex. The second message was certainly intended to keep SKVP guessing a little. Rex would have known that SKVP knew that he knew that they would see the message. It would keep them on their toes. Exciting times and better to come, if all went according to plan. Anyway he would know in a few days. It would be a distinguished prize to deliver back to SKVP who would certainly find ways of extracting the information which they felt could be useful to them. It would do wonders for his premium. This would put him in the major league; from now on he could ask almost any price for work and enjoy the luxury of picking only the jobs that took his fancy. Perhaps a week and it would be done. Meanwhile the sun was shining, the Adriatic at its most beguiling and Milena likewise. He enjoyed his sense of ownership. It amused him to know that George still lusted helplessly after her and he encouraged her to remove her bikini top when she sunbathed at sea since he knew it tormented the perspiring Englishman. Alex, now at liberty, did not appear to suffer in the same way but George's frustration was comfort enough for Peter who revelled in the power it gave him. He sucked noisily on his can.

In fact, if there was a cloud in his sky it took the shape of Alex. He was supposed to be a colleague and he owed his freedom to Peter, but his manner was formal, even distant. Peter knew that he had not approved of what had happened to Q but surely Alex had been around long enough to know that occasional killings were expedient in their business? Was he un assassin délicat? Surely not.

At least they had had no open disagreements. Alex seemed happy enough to go along with the idea of a lure for Rex. Perhaps it was just that the chemistry was wrong. You couldn't get on with everybody after all. It was probably the culture. After all, if he was honest, he felt no natural affection for the little Arab. What was he, Egyptian? Did they count as Arabs? He thought so. Politically, if not ethnically, as those disastrous six June days three years ago had shown. But, come to think of it, he couldn't think of anything he much liked about him. He was just a bit too clever by half, a real bloody intellectual, no balls obviously since Milena didn't do it for him, too small to be interested in sport. Christ even those bloody kaffirs at home showed real promise on the rugby pitch. What good was this fellow for anything? What the hell did SKVP see in him? What use was he? No balls.

He called to Milena, loud enough for George to hear. "How you doing, sweetie? I'm going for a lie down. You going to come too, help me sleep, hey? In due course?"

He stood up and moved towards the companion way.

Milena looked up from her deck chair.

"Okay, I'll be down in a minute."

"Better be quick. I've got a big urge. You don't want to miss it." He went heavily down stairs.

"Okay."

Milena saw George watching her over the top of his glasses. She shrugged and rolled her eyes.

"I think he will sleep without me," she said softly, mouthing the words.

"I hope so," said George to himself.

SEPTEMBER 23, WEDNESDAY
VENICE

They berthed on the Riva Sette Martiri, with its spectacular view of the basin, and went ashore to check the paper for messages Peter arranged to meet the others in a bar in Santa Croce, away from obvious tourist routes, and made his way to the international newsagent just off the Piazza San Marco. He would need to think carefully about his next message to Rex. It was important not to give him too much time to reflect; an imminent deadline would force him to make a decision. But he must be careful not to arouse suspicion by seeming to rush things. Three days, allowing him a day for travel, would be quite enough.

Assuming there was no message today, he would need to give the wheel a gentle shove.

He handed over an assortment of small coins and walked across the square, tucking the paper under his arm. The crowds of visitors had changed subtly over the last two weeks. There were fewer English and American voices to be heard now: French couples in their sixties, Dutch of course, and, beginning to reclaim their inheritance, Italians were returning after the summer evacuation. The sun was as high as ever but benign now that it had scarred the northern invaders and sent them on their way peeling and sore-footed. Within a week the rain likewise would return after its summer break. The city authorities would put out duckboard walks and hope that the tides would restrain themselves. The pigeons would not like it.

Peter unfolded the paper as he wove his way through the tourists and glanced down at the small familiar columns. It looked as though London was still pondering its move. No messages for Peter or SKVP yet so far as he could see. Then something made him stop so suddenly that a small man carrying a brown paper parcel cannoned uncontrollably into him.

"Scusi signore, no mi aspettavo che…" he began but Peter paid him no attention. He heard nothing except a curious tinnitus in his head. He brought the paper close to his eyes, squinting as the bright sun bounced painfully off the page. He had not been wrong. There was a message, an important one. But it wasn't for him.

> **Rex. Exchange details. Trieste September 26,**
> **Piazza dell'Unita d'Italia 23.29 hours. SKVP.**

Back on the boat he was not greatly reassured by the others' more measured reaction. George and Milena, of course, were not properly involved in the business and could not be expected to understand the implications. But Alex was curiously fatalistic, almost contemptuously so.

"Well you have been sending quite a few message in name of SKVP, no? You must not be surprise if they want send some of their own."

"Yes, but why now? Why interfere when I've got everything rolling along? Another week, they'll have the biggest goddam catch they've had in years. If they not careful they going to fuck the whole thing up. Especially now we don't have Q to exchange."

"I guess maybe that the point," said Alex quietly. "The muddier the water, the easier to get away with murder. Maybe SKVP want a little credit for themselves?"

"I am bloody SKVP!" said Peter hoarsely. "I'm as much a part of it as the bloody boss."

"And that may be boss's worry. Perhaps boss thinks it might look as if boss not doing enough. He worry about his reputation. He see someone else doing very good job. He feel the cold wind of your ambition blowing round his ankles. He muddy the water so he can go and hide in the swirl and work things out."

"Times like this," said Peter grumpily, "I just want to get back to the good old RSA and run my own affairs again.

It's the only way to be happy, making your own decisions, setting your own agenda, not being pissed on by a floorful of bosses who don't know the half of what their workers do and certainly don't appreciate it."

"Absolutely with you there, chum," said George, glad to see the conversation back on less contentious subject matter. "It's the only answer, work for yourself. That's when I was always happiest."

"I thought you did work for yourself," said Peter.

"Oh, I do. Just that, inevitably, you get one or two large customers who, jolly good, help you to keep the profits up but, because you need them, tend to make life hard for us. You know, huge orders of hard to source wines at no notice, that sort of thing. It's a tightrope between, on one hand, absolute independence with the risk of going broke and, on the other, the security blanket of regular buyers with the associated pressure they feel able to bring to bear."

"I see."

"Whereabouts in South Africa are you actually from?" he asked Peter, not very subtly.

"Cape Town. A little suburb called Muizenberg on the South Peninsula. Wonderful surfing. Very Jewish, falafels and bagels in the shops, a big synagogue. Jewzenberg they call it these days."

"So useful, the Jews," said Alex quietly, "the answer to everybody's problems. Whatever it is that goes wrong, you can always blame the bloody Jews."

"Well you should know, hey?" said Peter, not certain whether it was irony that he had detected in Alex's tone. "They certainly the reason for your little problems in Sinai.

Ah well, so Trieste then. A nicely-placed gateway between East and West. And closer to Milena's home. Did you know she was from Slovenia?"

SEPTEMBER 23
LONDON

It was raining, English weather at its most satirical. The morning had dawned clear, bright and mild, enough to cheer the hearts of those who were still coming to terms with the fact that it would be another forty-eight weeks before they could once again make a break for the sun. Half an hour in the park at lunchtime might even revive the fading tan, enough anyway for it to be admired sideways in the bathroom mirror tonight.

But at shortly after nine it had begun to rain, straight, remorseless, soaking rain. It rapidly flooded the gutters enough for taxi drivers to gain meagre satisfaction from their apparently heedless drenching of coatless pedestrians.

Rex stood by the window watching. A trickle of rain ran off the helmet of the policeman on duty at the gate below. He had no cape, umbrellas were not regulation issue. Rex imagined the steamy warmth of his uniform, the steady seepage of water through his shoulders and down his neck. He would be hoping that no visitors would come since to move would bring his arms and legs into chafing contact with the chill wetness of his uniform. Best course was to stay absolutely motionless.

The intercom buzzed on Rex's desk.

"Yes?"

"I have Mr Tenison for you. On green."

"Thank you." Rex picked up the green phone.

"Mr Tenison."

"Just returning your call, Rex. Good morning."

"You have, of course, seen the latest?"

"Yes, I have."

"And have you devised a recommended course of action?"

"Yes, I have, I think that, on the whole…"

"Good." Rex cut him off. "I have decided that we shall do nothing. We shall sit this one out for a few days. I want to see what Peter does."

"Just what I was going to suggest, Rex. I really do think we need to be very careful on this one."

"So do I."

SEPTEMBER 26 SATURDAY
TRIESTE

It had been an unforgettable evening, one that the tourists would recall long hence as they fingered their cluttered photograph albums. The rain had not come and the heat of the afternoon sun had warmed Trieste's old brick and marble so that it was possible to sit coatless on a café terrace beside the vast Piazza dell'Unita d'Italia and watch the sun drown itself in the oily water of the harbour. The ferries at Punto Franco Vecchio were keyed against the hectic swatch of pinks and reds. A seagull flew steadily, right on cue, the whole length of the waterfront before wheeling to disappear in the last fierce glare of reflected fire. The tourists had the grace to sit in silence, realising instinctively that any words of theirs could only reduce the imperial splendour of what they were seeing.

It had been rather lost on Peter who, having spent the evening in the bar of the Grand Hotel Duchi d'Aosta, had made his way by way of a service staircase up to the balustrade roof which commanded an excellent view of the piazza. But it was late September and, now that it was past eleven, it was cold. He had been there an hour, working on his usual principle that it was better to be in advance. Somewhere down there an SKVP agent was going through the ritual charade of the rendezvous. Perhaps, at one of the cafés, he had already submitted to the alfresco dinner, the offhanded waiter and the indifferent wine, because he knew he had to go through the motions of being an innocent tourist. The rules did not allow him simply to turn up in the piazza at twenty past eleven and seek out his contact. The absurd protocol, unwritten but devised by generations of gentleman agents, required him to expose himself well before the deadline. The other side would do the same and, over the course of time, the two agents would scan the piazza and, at length, identify each other. Perhaps, in the lee of the Molo Audace, a fast boat skulked, waiting for a speedy and untraceable getaway. Except that, since there was no Q, there would be no exchange and no getaway. He had told Alex to stay aboard and out of sight.

To Peter's right, the clock on the city hall showed eleven fifteen. If the hotel had not been so easy to access, the city hall would have been Peter's second option. He was relieved not to have had to spend an hour in that elegant but unaccommodating perch. Something would have to happen soon.

Twenty-five past, four minutes. It was a curious affectation of SKVP, thought Peter, to choose so pointlessly specific a time. Eleven thirty would have been as clear. It was a mark of waning professionalism that newer agents had begun to indulge in these whimsies. A sense of humour might be fine for fiction; the reality was duller and more mundane.

The old clock struck the half-hour and Peter shifted his position to lean as far out as he dared over the piazza.

There didn't seem to be any very obvious meeting going on, nor enough evidence of the little knot of men who would usually be lurking when an exchange was likely. He squinted as a man's figure walked diagonally across the piazza away from the hotel towards the café opposite. He walked purposefully, faster than a strolling tourist but more slowly than a local making his way home. There was something about him, a formality, a self-consciousness, almost a swagger although his height was hardly imposing. Peter swore and closed his eyes for a moment. It was Alex. Alex, walking brazenly past the most likely spot for the rendezvous, Alex who was meant to be under Peter's lock and key and apparently much-desired by both Britain and SKVP, Alex not just out but apparently doing his best to draw attention to himself.

Peter stared out, his gaze quartering the piazza for other potential players. Alex had vanished into the shadows on the other side and Peter stayed motionless for a further ten minutes, waiting for developments. He stiffened as two men appeared at the corner of the piazza. They strolled almost to the middle, quite near the café, whose waiters had just closed it for the night, and stopped. They were wearing dark suits and, if this had been a film, would probably have been wearing fedoras. One reached inside his jacket and pulled out a packet of cigarettes. He tapped it open on his hand and held it out to the other who took one. The first man looked behind him for a second and then, feeling in his trouser pocket, took out a lighter and lit both cigarettes. The two men spoke in low tones for a moment then shook hands and walked off in different directions. Neither looked back. There was silence in the piazza. Peter had begun to move when a door slammed suddenly in the stillness. He froze, holding his breath. He stared at the café, searching for a moment. There was nothing.

After a further ten minutes he levered himself gently back from the balustrade, ran down the service stairs and, finding the door back to the lobby, strolled to the front door and out into the night.

It was against procedure but anyway he walked towards the spot where Alex had disappeared and spent some time following the course he might have taken. Behind the piazza lay the bulk of the Teatro Verdi and beyond that a series of streets mostly made up of shops and bars, then a web of smaller alleys and side turnings. There was no one about. Occasionally, from an upper window, the shutters still open, he would hear a burst of conversation. Sometimes there was a shout but it was domestic stuff; the rendezvous had not happened. But how could it happen since SKVP did not have – and presumably were relying on Peter to produce Q – the chip with which they were bargaining? He sensed that events were sliding from his control; for the first time in months he felt almost baffled. It was curious not to know the rules, not to be the only one who knew the next move. For the moment someone else appeared to be setting the agenda and he couldn't think who it was. He felt impotent, frustrated and, almost, afraid.

When he got back to the yacht Alex was already there, leaning over the side.

"No joy then, my friend?" asked Alex as Peter climbed over the side, but Peter cut him off.

"What the bloody hell you playing at you stupid thick bastard?" he hissed. "You meant to be a fucking prisoner and you go walking about the square where any bugger can see you? You got to be bloody mad, man."

"Yes, anyone could see me," agreed Alex quietly. "But who knows who I am? No one has clue what I look like, mm? You didn't know who I was when you first pick me up, mm? Only people who know what I look like are SKVP and they know I'm with you anyway." He paused. "Don't they?"

Peter glared at him but said nothing.

"So it just seem worth having a look to see if I could see something from close range."

"Okay. You got a point I suppose. And did you see anything?"

"Nothing. But I wasn't expecting anything. Were you?"

"Not necessarily. You can never be sure. That's what this game is about, man. Second guessing."

"If you had not killed Q," said Alex very quietly. "He might have told you a lot about Rex. Now we know nothing, not even what he was up to."

"Q wasn't saying anything. That's the whole bloody point. He wasn't spitting so he was no bloody use."

"Not to you maybe. But then maybe your skill is not so good as interrogator. You are a good fixer but maybe you don't have the psychological skills."

"And you have?"

"Me? No, I don't think so. But we have whole departments of people – shrinks you would call them – who do nothing except study psychological warfare. For them even silence tell them something. They can work out what you hiding just by the way you don't answer their questions. I think even Q would not have kept them busy very long. They could have given us picture of his personality, how he might behave and so on. It might have been very useful. It might even have led us to Rex. But, never mind. You are the boss. And I'm sure you will have your own way to find out what is going on out there."

It was curious, George thought, how you could go off things. He remembered the bony nuns who had run his primary school going on about how material possessions were not just unimportant but were a definite hindrance. There had been something about camels he thought but he was a bit vague on that. He had not paid a great deal of attention at the time, largely because the moral seemed to be aimed at people who were thinking of entering the kingdom of heaven, something which did not then figure among his immediate ambitions. As such he had felt entitled to switch off since the lesson was clearly not meant for him. Nonetheless the effectiveness of the nuns' teaching methods, based as they were on simple attrition where constant repetition avoided the need for explanation, meant that even George had not avoided absorbing some of their messages. It was in his head, like an old library book, unused, only partially understood, but perfectly coded. In the same way he could, if anyone had asked him, recite the Confession, the Benedictus and much of the Te Deum with the blindly uncomprehending and unerring accuracy of an Italian singing an Elvis Presley number.

Anyway, going off things. When he had first come on board the Stavros Morgana, he had not been able to suppress a childish excitement about being on board a powerful yacht so obviously made for luxury. It was just his luck, he had thought, that the only time he got aboard a boat like this was in conditions where violence and fear

seemed the norm but, George being George, he had felt
that on the whole it was better to be aboard her in these
circumstances than not at all. What did life mean, after all,
without experience? That was how his luck worked out
and he was too used to it to spend time railing against it.
Same with Milena. The only way he was ever going to get
close to a fantastic thing like her was by being beaten up
and sexually teased but, given the choice, even the teasing
was better than using your imagination all the time.

Anyway, the yacht. It had seemed then the answer to a
young man's dream with its extensive decks, cabins with
real beds, its Habitat-furnished saloon; more like a London
studio than a mere boat. But, now that he had been on
board for nearly four weeks, he had begun to see its
limitations. The main problem, of course, was that there
was nowhere to go. Although big by the standards of any
pleasure-boat he had ever known, in comparison with a
house or flat, the Stavros Morgana was cramped. The
unspoken sense of imprisonment didn't help. It had
occurred to him that, now that Q was dead, he was as free
as Alex was since, so far as he could tell, Peter's links with
SKVP did not extend to handing George over to them. He
had, after all, offered to drop him off if he had wanted to
stay loyal to Q. On the other hand, how much validity did
that offer have? Probably not much, come to think of it.

Poor old Q. Perhaps he was well out of it. But somewhere,
he thought, a few thousand miles away in the Home
Counties, a woman in her late forties would be trying to
resist the urge to ring the office every day to ask if there
were news of her husband whose overseas posting had
unexpectedly been extended. She knew the rules, naturally;
she would not expect to have even a deliberately
innocuous postcard from him, but human nature being

what it was, the need to know something of what had happened to him and whether she needed to worry or not, was with her throughout the day, as she put clothes in the machine at home or dealt with colleagues at work. At night she seldom dreamed of him but would wake from a scenario in which someone had set her an ill-defined task which, though quite meaningless to her, almost certainly had enormous significance somewhere beyond her dream. She had the feeling that she had spent the whole night repeatedly but unsuccessfully striving to accomplish this elusive job. The sense of baffled failure usually conditioned her approach to the rest of the day.

Anyway, his apparent freedom. Well he was theoretically free, he supposed, to go at any time. And yet he was absolutely confident that any attempt to leave the boat on his own would produce questions from Peter. He could have left on the various occasions when Peter was away on some mission but he knew instinctively that he would feel hunted, probably justifiably, and that if ever Peter or one of his people should catch up with him, the jovial friendliness would not be much in evidence. In any case it seemed that his future was tied up with Peter until this particular mission was resolved one way or another. George had the strong feeling that things were coming to a head. Peter was evidently tense, no longer so obviously master of his circumstances. And that was another thing. It was funny how Peter had changed or was it that George had got to know him better? In the early days he had seemed strong, single-minded in a relaxed kind of way, almost heroic. Recently he had become jumpy and, astonishingly, indecisive. His South African roots had broken the surface more frequently both in his accent and in his unreconstructed treatment of Milena. He was drinking more.

Milena. Well that was another point. It looked as if she was finding the new Peter a little less appealing than the old version. Even George, famously and avowedly ignorant about how to behave with women, could see that she did not react well to Peter's boorishly suggestive invitations. A few weeks ago he would have had no need for such invitations; Milena was in his bunk as often as he wished, for she wished it too. Perhaps, as for all mercenaries, the essence of his life was the unpredictable, the constant change. Sitting out a sort of siege was not his style and he was chafing with frustration, urgent to be setting the pace, to be on the move again to the next mission, the next location, the next Milena. Probably she knew all this, perhaps she felt the same. Their allotted time together had run its span.

George was, against all reason, an optimist. Unkinder commentators would call him self-deluding. Either way, he had the spotted the cooling of the mercenary ardour and, with the instinct of an old dog, had wondered in an offhand way whether there might be an opening for him now. Not necessarily as a lover – he wasn't that deluded – but perhaps just as a companion. Of course he fancied Milena but he also liked her and would be happy simply to be her friend, especially as he could see that she too was feeling alone and had no one to talk to. Peter's teasing had stopped a few days ago: he had, almost automatically, winked at Milena when she stretched out in the sun and whispered hoarsely about her top. She had clicked her teeth.

"Oh no, Peter, I don't think this is funny any more." And had turned over on her tummy and closed her eyes.

George had mixed feeling about this. His first reaction was to be rather disappointed. Although now familiar with it, he still very much enjoyed admiring Milena's attractive young body. He did not think that this was something of which he would tire, as he had of the boat. He took in the view with all the quietly lustful enjoyment of a visitor to the Louvre. And, now that it had been curtailed he admitted to a sense of loss.

In the black and white film noir version of George's story this is where the juddering Korngold music swells more urgently and we see a series of dissolves between scenes of Peter pacing the deck, pussycat Buster asleep on Rex's knee, Alex looking quizzically out to sea, Peter pouring another drink, Tenison answering the phone, Peter fruitlessly scanning the small ads, Milena and George catching each other's eye and laughing quietly together, Rex's beringed finger pushing the desk intercom, Peter pouring another drink as Alex sneeringly mouths unheard jibes at him. And, superimposed over each dissolve, the pages of the calendar are ripped away by a powerful wind: September 25, 26, 27…

SEPTEMBER 28, MONDAY

Alex left the boat in mid-afternoon, as he regularly had over the last few days, saying he was going to walk into town.

"Okay, man. See you later." Peter called with unusual bonhomie. "Be careful."

Five minutes later he stood up and walked casually to the gangway at the stern. "Think I might go and see what's cooking too," he said to no one in particular. Milena, dozing under the awning amidships, gave no sign of having heard and he did not repeat himself.

Throwing his coat, unnecessary even for the fashion-conscious, over his shoulder, Peter strolled off.

Out of sight he quickened his pace and headed for the Piazza dell'Unita. He was pleased at the unaccustomed calm he felt. The days with no news, the increasing dislike he felt for Alex, a dislike now tinged with a curious unease, the unabated sense that he was no longer calling the shots, had all combined to shake his self-confidence. He felt constricted and purposeless and the answer, he had realised, was to take action, to force the pace and thus to re-establish control. The elation of a decision taken had put a spring in his stride as he headed for the piazza.

There were few people about, the hotel staff indolent, and it was easy for him to make his way to his look-out post on the roof. He laid his jacket carefully beside the balustrade, making certain that the side pocket was uppermost. He was sure that Alex would turn up in the piazza, if he wasn't already there. What the hell was the man up to? Something for sure, some Levantine double-dealing. Well today Peter was going to find out what it was and put a stop to it. He leaned his head against the balustrade, peering out onto the sunlit piazza. For God's sake, he was the man, he was the SKVP contact; he was the fellow running the show, keeping those conveniently confused links between SKVP and London. Who did Alex think was in charge? After all who had put a stop to Q's game? Why didn't Alex learn the lesson?

At length he saw what he had been waiting for. Alex walked into the piazza, sat down outside a café and ordered something. An espresso. Peter watched it arrive, waiting for the slightest signal from Alex to his contact. It must be that. He was meeting someone for a deal. But who? Who would Alex be doing deals with? He couldn't think, but he knew there was someone, it shouted from Alex's every move over the last few days. Alex fished in his pocket, left coins on the table and got up to leave. As he did so Peter breathed with satisfaction. A man had approached Alex. He looked like a tourist in his open shirt and blazer. Not bad, thought Peter. Better than the usual grey suit anyway. The man was talking to Alex who listened carefully. Peter knew that this was it. Time to put an end to Alex's double-dealing. He stretched an arm down to his coat and, from the side pocket, pulled out the pistol with which he had shot Q. Squinting through the balustrade he took a bead on Alex. Difficult to be certain from this distance, and the Makarov was hardly ideal for this kind of job, but even he would find it hard to stroll across a large piazza with a sniper's rifle. And pistols were fine for knocking off two-faced Arab shits like Alex. It would be good to be back in control. The two men were still talking. At any minute they might separate or walk off together to conclude whatever business they had in hand. Peter steadied the gun against the stone baluster, checked his aim, and squeezed the trigger. The crack was appallingly loud even on the roof but it could never have been heard from below. Peter did not hear the small cry that followed it but he could not have failed to pick up the long scream which trod on its heels. Looking down he saw three or four people gathered round a figure on the ground, among them a woman, still screaming as she fell to her knees beside it, waving her arms ineffectually. Peter stood up, trembling. Good that he had done it; should have done it long ago. He stooped to pick up his jacket and put the gun back in his pocket. As he turned to go he looked once more through the balustrade at the scene below. The woman was standing now, clutching a bundle in her arms while two men tried to comfort her. Peter heard police sirens approaching. He stopped. The fallen figure had disappeared; that was a puzzle. But what froze him was the realisation that one of the men comforting the woman was Alex. He looked back at the woman. The bundle. Oh shit. He had shot a child.

He made his way quickly down through the hotel and back to the boat. In the confusion in the piazza, no one took any notice of him. He tried to calm himself as he walked. Where did the woman and child appear from? What were they doing? He simply hadn't noticed them, so intent was he on Alex. And there would be other questions. Where had he been, when they asked? Just for a walk? Where did he go? Oh just along the docks; nowhere near the Piazza.

If Milena or George noticed him return they gave no sign. There had been pretty little conversation between them anyway for some days now and their former banter was just a memory. Peter went below and lay on his bunk. He failed to doze and spent a fitful half hour trying to understand what he had done. Perhaps explanation and even justification might then follow. He was not wholly unsuccessful.

Sometime later he heard Alex arrive back and noticed fretfully that the others greeted him cheerfully. Alex back. Oh shit. He couldn't stand it.

At supper that night Alex asked Peter if he had been into town too.

"Well yes, I did actually, if that's all right with you," Peter replied heavily.

"None of my business what you do, Peter," said Alex. "I just wonder whether you heard the trouble in the piazza?"

"Trouble?"

"It was rather unpleasant. I had been to see the cathedral – even Muslims can appreciate Christian art by the way – and I went for a coffee on the piazza on the way back. As I leaving a man come up and ask me the way to the Hotel Continentale. Typical of course that he should pick another tourist. In fact someone else had already given him wrong directions and he hoping I know the way. As it happens I did because I pass it the other day – it's in the via San Niccoló – and I just starting to explain – my Italian not so good – when there comes this little cry. I didn't notice at once but straightaway a woman start screaming. We turn round and there was this little boy, perhaps six or seven years, lying on the ground. Lot of blood. I thought he must have fallen and stunned himself, he was so still. But the woman say no he just fell as if he had been shot. And she right. When we lift him up there's a small hole in his head and big one on the other side. He was dead even before I see him. Terrible."

"Christ," said George breathing out. "Who the hell kills a child? And where was the bloke with the gun? Did you get a look at him?"

"No. No one in sight. I don't know where he was. But the piazza was quite empty. You know, middle of the afternoon, only a few tourists, so it would be hard for him to lose himself in a crowd."

Milena was pale, staring at Alex and holding the edge of the table. "But you ask the right question. Who kills a child?"

"I have been thinking," said Alex, "and I can only think they didn't mean to kill child. A mistake. They meant to kill someone else. Someone close to the child. Maybe the Mafia. What you think, Peter? You know anything about the Mafia?"

"Not a thing. Never had anything to do with them, thank God. But hey that was a bad turn for you. I'm sorry."

"Don't be sorry for me, Peter. Be sorry for the little boy. And for his mother who has lost her son. And who will have to tell his father tonight. 'Que c'est triste, Venise' They were playing that in the café. Very appropriate."

SEPTEMBER 30, WEDNESDAY
TRIESTE

The rain had come. It swept like damp gauze across the piazza, grey and clinging. It roughened the surface of the oily puddles and drizzled from the faded blinds of the few shops which were open. Peter had walked, as he had every day this week, to the newspaper shop, with decreasing hope of any message. He admitted to himself now, that he was defeated. He simply could not come to terms with the total silence from Rex and he had still not worked out why SKVP should have intervened so suddenly, nor so uniquely. And without involving him. After all, they knew he was on the case. Perhaps that was exactly why they hadn't contacted him – and what did that mean for him? He would have been glad to hear from them now. He had toyed with sending another message himself but did not pursue the idea, thinking that it might show that he was rattled. His confidence had gone and he knew that his rise to the premier league was an evaporated dream. He felt that he had had enough of being the pace-setter. He wanted to be away, taking simple orders, carrying out simple functions, somewhere warm.

The shopkeeper hardly looked up from his crossword as Peter poured a handful of small coins into his outstretched hand. Peter stood for a moment in the doorway, tossing up whether to check the ads now in the dry and postpone the squelching walk back to the boat. He compromised and went into the café two doors down and ordered a ristretto. He was the only customer; it was 3.30 and a Wednesday. While the machine gurgled he folded his paper back and drew his eye wearily to the back page. Nothing, nothing, lonely hearts, colonic irrigation, double-barrelled girls seek similar to share flat in Queensgate. The coffee came and he absent-mindedly slid more silver across the counter. He raised the cup. It was another classic cinema cliché. At the precise moment of his first mouthful a number of things happened: his eyes widened in disbelief, he choked and spat coffee over the page and put the cup down so fast that it spilt the rest of the coffee in a steaming puddle over the marble counter from where it began to drip onto his already soaking deck shoes. He leapt back from the counter but, without thinking, put his paper on the counter to read again what he had seen. In an instant the paper had absorbed the residue of his coffee and had assumed the consistency of, well, wet newspaper. As the brown stain spread like an advancing army through the airmail paper, Peter could nonetheless make out the wording of the new message. He had not been mistaken.

Rex. Q ok. Make contact Villach. Require warm clothing. Peter.

Confronted with serious injury the body produces its own endorphins – natural painkillers which keep the victim in a state of calm until doctors can administer extended doses of morphine. Perhaps, in cases of severe mental shock, a sort of drip-feed of amnesiac valium can numb the brain until it has time to deal with the problem. Whatever the truth, Peter remembered nothing of his stumbling run back to the boat, nor his mad shouts for his colleagues as he blundered aboard. He came to his sense only when he found himself across the table in the saloon from Alex and Milena. George hovered near the doorway. Peter could hear himself shouting but he couldn't make out what he was saying.

"Who put the ad in?" he heard Alex say quietly. "Well let us try to work it out, mm? Not you, Peter, you say? Okay. Not Q because he is dead. George? Unlikely. Milena? Never. SKVP maybe? Well, it's possible. So who does that leave, Peter, mm?

Peter stared at him.

"You? You put the ad in?"

Alex smiled.

"You going to tell me why?"

"What reason I have for writing to Rex? Let us examine. First, because nothing happening. You have been the commander on this operation, you have made the decisions, we have done what you told us. You told us you need to get Rex out here. But he hasn't come and maybe we have got tired of waiting. So, one reason might be to, as you would say, move things on. It's a very nice boat, of course, but we all have lives to lead. Winter is coming. If I think you have lost the battle with Rex then maybe I think of putting in ad which change the story a little."

Peter stared at him, focussing with difficulty on the little Egyptian.

"But Christ, man, you right. I am the boss. Why not talk to me before you start interfering?"

"Because you no longer the boss. You have lost control. And I have assumed it."

Peter lunged across the table towards Alex who slid his chair easily back out of reach.

"You? Since when?"

"Since some days ago when I contact SKVP from Rimini to tell them we are in Trieste on the 23rd."

"You telling me you put that message in too?"

"Who else? SKVP needed to know what going on since you seem to be losing track."

"But I work for SKVP. I am bloody SKVP!"

"Not according to them. I know times are hard but do you think it likely that SKVP would use someone with your record? We need people with brains, with cunning, people who can think before they act."

He paused.

"Not gun people down in the street. Especially not children."

"You accusing me of that?"

"Not unless you want me to. I make general point not a specific one. My point is that we need spies not gangsters or mercenaries."

"Mercenaries? Who says I'm a mercenary?"

"Your record does, Peter. I know it well since I took some time to learn it. Schoolboy member of the Broederbond, service in Central Africa, in Bangui in 66 for the overthrow of David Dacko. Remember Sharpeville? Of course you do. You were there, weren't you, loosing off at the blacks? A move into the Balkans to cover your tracks, undercover action with the Serbs against Tito, a chance meeting with Pyotr who sees the usefulness of a not every clever agent who speaks English. Good potential there as a double, mm? I think Pyotr chose well. His plan to use you to 'rescue' George from SKVP was inspired. And to use George to get Q out. Pity we never had a chance to find out from Q what George is really there for. And that's what give you away, Peter. Spies wait forever, if necessary. Mercenaries kill. By the way, George told me you ask him what he does down in Beirut. Nice try. But it suggests to me an underestimation of British intelligence. Do you really think they would allow George to know what his usefulness is?"

George shifted against the doorpost. He couldn't decide if it was his pride or his life which was most at risk.

"So, without Q," went on Alex, "it becomes very important to tempt out Rex. But that's a very different idea. That's something for spies, not mercenaries."

"Why don't you shut up about mercenaries, you little gyppo bastard! Peter shouted suddenly. "I'm not here to be lectured about spying by you."

"No, you are right. It would be a waste of my time. But I was explaining why SKVP would never recruit you as anything except a foot-soldier – cheap and expendable. And now that you have over-reached yourself by trying to get hold of Rex, maybe you can see why. Now I have taken over the project and we shall see, some of us, whether we can't attract him to Villach by a call for help rather than by empty threats."

"Villach! Where the hell is that? And why would we want

to go there?"

"You don't. It's the rest of us who want to go. But don't worry, you will stay here in Trieste."

"To do what?"

"Well, Peter, to die."

Peter sat back hard against the cabin wall. The thin wood bowed slightly under the weight of his broad back.

"What does that mean?" he asked with a forced laugh.

"I read once about the last words of a British prime minister, Lord Palmerston, when his doctor told him he was going to die. He said 'Die, dear doctor? That's the last thing I shall do.' Clever isn't it? And so unusual to be witty in the face of death. I think you will understand what I mean by die when I tell you that I forgot to mention another little bit of your history that I discovered. You did a little work last year for a firm called Mossad, am I right? It seems you were even involved in what happened in the Sinai Peninsula. Did you really think that even a silly old Egyptian would not find out about that? That has been your trouble, Peter. You have worked for big firms but you have made the mistake of believing that you were big too. But big firms use hundreds of little people who are, in the end, dispensable; there are very few stars. You not a star. And you are dispensable. The Egyptians and SKVP are working closely on how to put right what happened in 67 and we shall simply walk on anything or anyone who gets in our way. You have got in our way and now I shall walk on you."

Peter began to shout in wild, animal roars, pressing himself further and further back into the plywood wall, straightening his muscular arms against the edge of the table. As the wood began to crack, he lunged at Alex. There was a small pop and a sudden silence as Peter's roars ceased for a moment. He stared at Alex in disbelief.

"Jesus," he said, "you shot me."

"Yes, but only in the foot," said Alex. He brought his hands from under the table revealing a small, silenced black pistol. "But now I am going to shoot you in the head. Unless you can get away. I shall give you a start. I will count to three. One."

The table finally gave way to the force of Peter's lunge and the big man shouted in pain as he put his weight on his left foot which, George saw, was bleeding heavily. He moved quickly aside as Peter burst out of the door and up the little ladder.

"Two," Alex called after him.

There was a kind of grisly conga as George and Milena followed Alex on deck. Peter had nearly reached the gangplank.

"Three," said Alex quietly. There was another pop and Peter slipped clumsily onto his face. George and Milena watched as the steady rain soaked his shirt and began to dilute the thin trickle of blood which ran from beneath his head and down the grey-brown decking. Milena began to sob to herself and George, who was shivering nervously, put an arm round her shoulder. She buried her head in his chest. George wondered anxiously how sweaty he smelled. He watched Alex who was still standing at the top of the companionway and wondered dully whether he was going to shoot them too.

Alex seemed to understand for he smiled. "Time to pack, my friends," he said. "If we are going to Villach, we should start soon."

George looked back at the bundle of what had been Peter.

"Leave him," said Alex. "He's best where he is."

NINE

LIVERPOOL

Andrew had known that he would regret going back to the Adelphi cocktail bar. He had known that it would do nothing but revive memories of their meetings there but – he smiled grimly as one did in these circumstances, remembering what Lesley had said about needing to be sad – the pain was better than the numbness. And pain there was, as sharp and unremitting as ever. It had, still, the effect of dulling his appetite for almost everything else in his life. He had known nothing to alleviate the ache. He felt spiritually, mentally and physically unhealthy; he disliked other people, took no joy in music or books, save for the few special tunes which resonated with the pain of memories of their time together. A trio was playing, the pianist strolling dreamily over his keyboard, but it sounded metallic and charmless. Even the bar, which had once seemed so welcoming and cleverly designed, now exuded hostility; the atmosphere of friendly intimacy which had perfectly reflected his own excitedly self-confident passion now felt harsh. The configuration of the room was disjointed, its former proportions misshapen and imbued with a crude irregularity as if they were the set for an obscure German Expressionist film. The chairs where they had sat together were unforgiving and ugly; the big mirror on the wall leered at him and each framed picture now carried an insult. The high ceiling, formerly so elegant, now stared down at him in icy disdain; contempt seeped from the walls. The drummer dragged his brushes with world-weary cynicism across his snare-drum, flicking his hi-hat with careless disinterest.

I feel so lonely
Just for you only…

OCTOBER 1, THURSDAY
SLOVENIA

The road from Trieste was under construction. The Yugoslavs had decided that it would be helpful to their tourist industry to have a motorway from Trieste to Ljubljana. Work had started in the spring and was the first stage was to be completed within two years. Meanwhile, drivers heading into Slovenia had to make do with the elderly 409 highway, whose concrete slab construction set up a percussion through the car which, in spite of its regularity, was unsettling and impossible to get used to.

George and Milena sat together in the back of the not very big Alfa which Alex was driving. They had followed him, like small obedient dogs, as he calmly pointed at their cabins and told them to get ready to leave. Neither had much to bring. George had still only the basic kit in the suitcase with which he had left Beirut a month ago. A month? It felt like… Milena, similarly, was used to travelling light and had a small holdall and beach bag. It took only moments to get their stuff together and they were soon ashore, stepping past Peter's body with the now practised ability to ignore what they did not choose to see.

Alex had somehow found a taxi which had taken them to a

garage on the outskirts where the Alfa was waiting. It was clear that they were expected and, in a very few moments, they were on their way.

Milena was silent, apparently overcome by fatigue and shock. George was tired too but he wanted to talk. He was surprised that Milena had not been hysterical when Peter had been shot. She did not seem the sort of girl who could have seen much killing and certainly not one who would ever become immune to it, however much she saw. George would have expected any murder, especially one as chilling as Peter's, to have had a profound effect on her. After all they were lovers. How long had she known him? How could she take his death so apparently calmly? These were things he could not ask her. One day perhaps but not now.

He leaned over the passenger seat. "Why Villach?" he asked.

Alex looked back at him over his shoulder.

"It's close, it's Austria, so fairly neutral. SKVP safe house. We'll be in a safe suite inside the hotel. Very unobtrusive. It's the sort of place someone like Rex would feel happy about coming out to. Trieste was always wrong. Too much atmosphere, too many Yugoslavs. To an Englishman it feels like bandit country I would think, mm?

"But why Villach? I mean, will it mean anything to Rex? I never heard Q mention anything about it. Not that I would have anyway, come to think of it. Q didn't tell me more than half of what he absolutely had to, and Austria was miles out of my territory."

"If Rex is interested enough in getting Q back, he'll go anywhere. But I think he is more likely to feel tempted by Villach. That's all. Also it convenient being on the border of three countries. If there's trouble there's a greater choice of places to run."

"How will Rex know where to find us?"

"Like SKVP he has people everywhere. It not take them too long to hear about three recent arrivals. "

George sat back in the cramped Alfa. Milena, who had been hunched looking vacantly out of the window, straightened and leaned back alongside him. She laid her head on his shoulder. George was delighted but apprehensive. It was almost the nicest thing he knew to have this beautiful girl nestled beside him. But he knew that, in a few minutes, he would have to move. He was constitutionally incapable of sitting still for longer. How appalling, he thought, to want so very much to do something and simply not be able to do it. He tried to relax.

Now that the past seemed, as it were, pretty much behind him, now that Peter was dead, Peter who had rescued him – if it had been a rescue – from SKVP, what was the future? Was he now Alex's prisoner, on his way to interrogation by SKVP? Alex had made no move to threaten him, had not needed to, he thought, since his elimination of Peter had been the directest demonstration of his control of the situation. The thought of interrogation was a worry and yet a limited one since, having absolutely nothing to hide, he would not have the problem of trying bravely to conceal any secrets.

And what of Milena whose warmth pressed firmly against his left side and reminded him sooner than he would have liked that his left leg was about to go to sleep and that he absolutely must move it. It was a pity to break the spell but he had no choice. As delicately as he could manage, he straightened his aching leg and raised his left arm above Milena's head, intending to turn away from her so that she could lean against his back. As he did so however Milena turned in towards him, buried her face drowsily in his chest and put her arm round his waist. She sighed deeply like a sleeping child. George let his arm drop casually around her shoulder. It was not, after all, so uncomfortable.

They crossed the border early in the evening and Alex drove them to the Carinthia hotel beside the river in Villach. He checked them into a three-room suite. "Sleep well." He said. "Take tomorrow easy. Let's talk the day after."

OCTOBER 1, THURSDAY

The Times

Yacht for sale, berthed Trieste. SKVP.

At around half-past one the next day, which turned out to be on bright sunshine, George ate lunch on his balcony overlooking the Drava and the Karnic Alps beyond.

Alex joined him.

"Refreshed?"

"Much better, old chum, thank you."

He poured Alex a glass of wine. "Carinthian. I think you'll like it. Quite delicate after the slight heftiness of the Musar."

He watched while Alex drank.

"If you don't mind my asking, what's the order of play now then? Any clues?"

Alex smiled. "It mostly a question of waiting, I'm afraid. And tidying up loose ends."

"Such as?"

Alex unfolded the paper he had brought with him. It was the Times. "About halfway down in the second column."

George examined the familiar back page, running his eye down the assortment of ads. At length he nodded in recognition.

"That's pretty final, isn't it? What will they make of that?"

"SKVP will know that I have concluded the Peter operation and that I am still waiting for Rex. Rex will hope it means that SKVP found the yacht too late – just after the first Villach message – and that Q is safe here with Peter. But the only way to be sure is to come and see for himself."

"How would he know where to come?"

"He would suggest a rendezvous somewhere."

"And if he doesn't?"

"Then he won't come, he has lost Q and for all of us the operation has not been a complete success."

"Success? Speaking as a very junior cog I can't think of anything that's happened that anyone could claim was a success."

"No, you are right. If we still had Q then we should be on our way to some useful intelligence. But without him what do we have?"

"Not much."

"We have you."

George swallowed. "I was afraid you'd say that. Of course you do. But, as you must realise by now, I don't seem to know very much."

"I believe you. But someone somewhere knows something about you and, one day, we will find out. It may take a long time, unless Rex grace us with a visit but, as I say to Peter, a true agent is happy to play the long game."

"How long will you wait for Rex?"

"I think two weeks will be enough."

OCTOBER 5, MONDAY
LONDON

It was a relief when Tenison's phone rang. The message from Peter in Villach had raised great hopes after the week of silence but the further silence which had followed it had been all the more depressing. The news that Q was safe had lifted spirits but his subsequent failure to report in had been puzzling because so out of character. The thought that was now beginning to form in the department's mind was that the Villach message had not perhaps been all it had seemed. The warm clothing – a coded cry for reinforcements – suggested that there had been serious problems, but until Q himself got in touch with specifics of an rv or the nature of the help they needed, there was little that they could deduce. SKVP's message about the yacht had meant nothing either way. Rex had taken the decision to face out whatever threat it might pose. There was no virtue, everyone agreed, in his plunging into already muddy waters. If Q were there he would, somehow, find a way to get in touch.

As Tenison had guessed, it was Rex on the phone.

"That's a week with no word, Mr Tenison," came that smooth voice.

"Yes, Rex."

"I think it may be time to take some small action, I am very much afraid that we have lost Q. But – in the hope that I'm wrong – I should like to reassure him or whoever he might be with that, from our point of view, the file is still open. Will you send him something appropriate?"

"Right away, Rex."

"And, if there's no reply within two days, repeat it."

Tenison knew, with all the experience his five years in the service had given him, with all the naiveté he retained, that Q was finished. He had no reason to know, and that was just the point. It was the instinctive, almost telepathetic sense which one twin feels for another, that brought him to know that he would never see Q again. He felt a cavernous sense of loss for, although he had never found Q warm, he respected his basic humanity. And it was simply as a man, and vulnerable, that he thought of him now, in all his nakedness, a man who had once been a little boy, who had grown up, become an adult but who, for all the sophistication which responsibility had lent him, was still a human, a brother, a father, a husband. Tenison sighed inwardly as he thought of the family. They will have to be told. He got up and went to the window. Not at once of course. A trickle of non-committal pre-written postcards would come from overseas postboxes but, at length, when the time was right – no doubt after his wife had realised the truth for herself – someone would go and see her and explain, soberly, that Q had had an accident and would not be returning. He hoped to God it wouldn't be him. Unlikely in fact. They usually tried to keep it impersonal by sending someone who had never known him. Poor Q. Poor family. It was unspeakable that he should just disappear and that they should never know, never be allowed to know the truth of how he died. Tenison leaned his head against the glass and closed his eyes.

Rex had put the phone down as carefully as usual and with the same certain knowledge as Tenison that they were playing out a ritual farce. Tenison's message would never be read, at least never by Q. Rex sighed. It was hell losing people. Q had been a good operator, had run his department with unostentatious flair, always thought ahead. They had known each other for years, never close but familiar. Rex wondered whether Q had had any inkling that he might get into trouble. Probably not. He had not been a coward but years of awareness of the need for economy of engagement would have given Q a profound sense of caution, of the importance of avoiding an unnecessarily high profile. One would have to write, in due course, to his wife. She was, Rex remembered, something of a church-goer. Something patriotic perhaps but with a philosophical touch; St Francis perhaps. Where there was discord, Q had brought peace, that sort of thing…

Rex stood and strode to the window. Elegant fingers held back the gauze curtain revealing the view upriver. Westminster. That was the future. Now that we were back in power there might be opportunities to make a real difference.

OCTOBER 6, TUESDAY

The Times

Q at Villach. Your report overdue. Rex.

Alex brought the paper the next day and showed them Rex's message.

"He is interested. But how interested, mm? Another week will tell us."

The Austrian weather remained benign and, to his own surprise, George found himself going for walks in the foothills. There was something almost English about the thick green of the fields and the gentleness of the slopes. And yet, in a way he couldn't define, he knew that it was different. It wasn't just the obvious things like the wayside crosses or even the clothes the local people wore, it was vague but unmistakeable. Even the cows looked different.

Milena took to coming with him. She asked him about his home life, what he had been doing in Beirut before all this. At first he was cautious for, although he was very fond of her, he wasn't certain that she wasn't teasing him or even – this would have been a pretty desperate last throw – trying to ease facts out of him for SKVP. In the end he let himself be convinced by her evident seriousness and, as the days went by, he told her more about his childhood in Brentwood, his mother's death when he was eight, his time in the army, the necessity imposed on him by his dad of making his own way. He told her how he had at length found something like contentment in Beirut – "although I don't think I've got it in me to be really bloody miserable"

– away from what he saw as the increasingly unfamiliar place that was Britain, with his wine and his trips to the Beka'a, his small circle of not very close friends.

When he asked Milena about her own background she shook her head. "Much to tell."

Over the days she told him a few details. Born in a small village north of Ljubljana just towards the end of the war. For people in eastern Europe of course there had been no VE Day, no liberation. For many Tito and his partisans, strongly backed by Stalin, were quite as much of a threat as the Nazis. Thousands of Slovenes tried to escape the pincer and reach Allied troops coming up through Italy. Those who made it were lucky. Others, like Milena's parents, made for Austria because it was much nearer. The British in Austria were under orders not to upset Tito. The refugees were promised free passage to Italy, but, treacherously, in May 1945, were in fact returned to Slovenia, often in filthy, suffocating cattle wagons. Tito saw the refugees as a threat and between seven and eleven thousand of them were executed on their return. In a rare moment of humanity, the partisan leader, seeing no sense in killing babies, had arranged for children to be taken to local churches before their parents were shot. The priests had had somehow had to find foster homes for the orphans and Milena grew up, like many hundreds of her contemporaries, with adopting families. Her own new parents had given her the same love and affection as their other daughter but had been scrupulous, when she was eighteen, in telling her the truth about her origins.

Milena had reacted calmly to the news. Because of her close relationship with her new parents, it seemed like someone else's story, nothing with which she could identify.

It had come back to her with great clarity on the drive from Trieste.

Slovenia was by some way the most relaxed of the countries in the Yugoslav republic, itself the least repressive of the soviet empire. Tito, as George knew, was well-regarded by the West largely because of his valuable war service, and regarded western tourism as an efficient source of hard currency.

Milena went to university in Ljubljana, improved the English she had already learned from American films and music. She was introduced to *Mladina*, the alternative political and cultural magazine and began little by little to be radicalised. Despite Slovenia's comparatively benign regime, she felt a primitive urge to revolt. No doubt, viscerally, this had much to do what she now knew about her past and was fermented by the excitement of growing up and discovering the absolute ambition of youth. While she never joined any group or espoused any single creed, she was consumed by a passion to break away, to destroy something, maybe rebuild something else, she didn't know what. Thus, when she had been on holiday with a student group to Trieste and had met a well-made blond South African in a bar, she had recognised this as a good enough way of doing whatever it was she was going to do. Peter was strong, decisive, sexy and had connections which enabled him to travel freely, if discreetly, through the Balkans. For over three years she had spent time with Peter, sometimes on boats, sometimes travelling in powerful cars into other countries. She knew that what he did was counter-legal and subversive though each was careful not to discuss the details. For her, each trip with Peter was an extended holiday which made bearable each return to Ljubljana and a succession of temporary waitressing jobs. She had, she supposed, known that it was going nowhere. It had fed her hunger for excitement and revolt but, even before Peter's unpredicted implosion, she had know that she would have to break out and find a life for herself. Things were changing in Yugoslavia. Even the great Tito could not last forever; he was nearly eighty now and she wanted to be in a position to affect what happened when he died. It was time perhaps for that political affiliation which she had always avoided.

"And you. Will you go back to your friends in Beirut?"

"I don't suppose a single one of them has even wondered where I am, let alone do anything about trying to find out if I'm all right. But I don't really need friends, not close ones, I suppose. I'm not what they call a loner, mark you. I love company. But I guess I've never had anyone to depend on so I've never felt the need."

"And you never wanted to get married? You had girl friends at least in England?"

"Not since I was a boy. Can't say I haven't thought it would be rather nice, you know. But there you are. It never happened. I'm not much good in the chatting up department. As you well know," he said, happy not to feel the usual flush of embarrassment. Some things were improving anyway.

At dinner in the hotel that evening, Milena asked George again about Beirut.

"Do you want to go back?"

"Well I think I would but, as you know, I don't think it's for me to make any plans at the moment. I think old Alex here is pretty much the master of ceremonies. I've always been the sort of bloke who got told what to do basically. I don't much care for it but I don't much mind either and it seems to be the way people prefer to do it. So, when he tells me whatever he's got lined up I'll probably do it or go there. Whatever."

"But would you like to go back?" asked Alex.

"On the whole, yes. Lebanon is a very beautiful country, the people are generally obliging, it has a kind of European feel to it, the wine-trade is a good one to be in, even with the added complication of all the Q business. I had thought of looking into the Balkan market. I was beginning to hear good things about their stuff. Bulgarian wine? May sound a bit odd but if it's good your ordinary punter might give it a whirl. The Soviets would probably subsidise the price in the interest of some hard currency."

"I'm very glad to hear that," said Alex, "because I think SKVP would like you to go back."

"And start again?"

"Of course, start again."

George chuckled appreciatively. "I like your style, Alex, I must say. I remember what you said about the long game. So I just go back, pick up the pieces and wait to see what happens?"

"Precisely. And we will wait to see what happens. And perhaps, one day, someone from the embassy will call on you and ask for your help. And perhaps then we shall find out why it is that the British want you there. I have my own suspicions, of course, but I should like to know for sure."

"And they are?"

"Oh, that you are there for the sole purpose of keeping SKVP guessing. The packages are irrelevant, unimportant.

What matters is that there seems to be activity, something going on which SKVP does not understand. You are a diversion, a kind of rogue pawn, without power but significant because it makes SKVP wonder what, one day, you might be called on to do."

"Same thought crossed my mind. If we're right, they haven't done too badly so far, have they?"

"No, but at what a cost. That's a big price to pay to keep up a bluff."

George was silent as he thought about his own terrors and the impersonal killings of Q and Peter. He sipped his Niersteiner.

"So the answer is just to go back and open up again?"

"Yes. SKVP will subsidise you discreetly for some time and, then maybe in a month or so if London haven' t been in touch, you can put a little ad in the paper for Rex. 'Holiday over; business as usual'. Something like that."

"Normal service will be resumed as soon as possible."
"Very good. Do you think you will be able to convince Rex that you were just an innocent hostage all along?"

"Not even sure that Rex knows I exist. I was really there for Q. But I've never had any problem convincing people I'm a blithering silly-arse. I think I could probably persuade Rex."

"And of course you will be discreetly useful to SKVP in Beirut."

"Beirut," said Milena quietly. "You will be happy to be home again."

"Have you ever been there?"

She paused. "Yes. I was there once for a meeting. With

Peter. But the other people didn't show up. It's a very exciting city."

"Would you like to go back?"

"Very much." She looked at him.

George looked back. The tremble in his legs seemed to have returned.

"Do you know what I'm thinking?"

"No. What?" flirtatiously.

"Why don't you come with me?"

"George, I knew you were a romantic. I would love to come to Beirut. But there is a little problem."

"Usually is."

"You are a very nice man but I don't desire you as my lover. So I do not think it would work to spend my life with you."

"Fair enough," he said. It's always good to be told straight out." He took a drink.

"I suppose there's no chance you'd settle for a year or so? A month maybe? Only joking."

She said nothing but smiled.

"Looks like it's just one ticket for Beirut then, Alex."

He was used to keeping up a brave front but he was shocked to realise how flat he suddenly felt. Had he really allowed himself to think that all that friendly chat was a come-on? Grow up, George. Be your bloody age.

"Well in two days we shall go," said Alex who had watched the exchange sympathetically over his coffee. "Our two weeks are up. We shall not see Rex this time. So today

SKVP will have read my final message which will explain that the mission is over and that the three of us are leaving. I will wait for a reply and then I shall go to Cairo to see my mother. SKVP will think I am bringing you to them but, in due course, I will explain to them why it was better that you should go home. You will hear from me. Not through the Times. We have other means. But you will hear."

"And you, Milena, since you've turned down Beirut?"

"Back to Slovenia to see my family. And to see if I can help my country find a future for itself."

OCTOBER 8, THURSDAY

The Times

> Q at Villach. Repeat your report overdue. Rex.

OCTOBER 14, WEDNESDAY

The Times

> SKVP. Book 3 rooms at hotel. Alex.

OCTOBER 15, THURSDAY

The Times

Alex. Direct contact soonest. SKVP.

OCTOBER 16, FRIDAY

The Times

Rex. Warm clothing missing. No trace of Q or party. The girl in red.

And there, it seemed, the messages ended. Over the next few days Andrew searched the column but there was no further sign of any communication. The project, whatever it had been, had come to a rather wistful end. It had been, he thought, not unlike a love affair: excitement, novelty, a bit of danger; apparent triumph and a confident breakthrough; then betrayal, deception, disappointment and a grey petering out to an uncertain conclusion. All he had to do now was write the end of George and Milena, Alex and Tenison whom he would see no more.

What he really wanted to write was a letter to Lesley now that they had been apart for some time, weeks without seeing or speaking to each other. He wanted to tell her how he didn't really miss her at first because she was so much a part of his life that he seemed almost to carry her with him wherever he went, seeing everything that he saw. But then, he wanted to say, that gave way to the kick in the stomach every time he realised that she wasn't there. He had never known companionship like it – such easy, relaxed friendship and affection. And without it was to be without humour or smiles or enthusiasm. He wanted to talk to her again, to say that there was nothing now but a daily endless drift, the wish that time would pass more quickly so that either he could see her again or, since this was improbable, to resolve to himself that she was finally gone and let the scar tissue form. If she could simply see the depth of his sadness she would surely recognise how embedded she was in his life and come to his rescue, telling him softly that it had all been a mistake. But he knew that it didn't work like that.

OCTOBER 16, FRIDAY
LONDON

For most people, however much they enjoy their job, leaving the office for home lifts the spirits, never more than on a Friday. Tenison was no exception. He ran down the wide carpeted stairs, through the oddly austere lobby and out into the cool autumn air. Turning along the embankment he headed for the Underground. His good mood was tempered by his recurring reflections on Q, his disappearance and all that that could mean. Was it really possible that he had come up against an immovable force, had fallen into a trap, and utterly uncharacteristically misjudged a situation?

Every deputy at some time or another feels that he could

do his boss's job better than his boss and there had been times recently when Tenison had longed to counter Q's reserved caution with a more adventurous approach. He wondered now whether that would have made any difference; after all Q had taken the undoubtedly courageous decision to put himself on the front line. And to what effect?

What might Tenison have done differently? And, more to the point, what might he do now? Perhaps, he thought with a twinge of guilt, this was his moment. With Q gone who would take things on? He had the sense that Rex regarded him favourably, had always appeared to listen to him. The story wasn't dead even if the trail had gone cold. There was still more to discover about what role Alex had really played. And Peter; his message had said that Q was ok but Tenison and probably Rex doubted this. So who was Peter and could they continue to trust him? These were things Tenison felt emboldened to raise with Rex on Monday; who knew where that might lead?

As he trotted across the road dodging the home-going traffic, he felt his wristwatch come loose and fall to the ground. Cursing, he stopped abruptly and, without thinking, turned back to pick it up. The driver of the approaching Volvo had seen what had happened and slowed down, stopping just short of the fallen watch. Tenison knelt to collect the watch and waved warmly to the driver who had avoided flattening both it and himself. The driver raised a hand in acknowledgement and Tenison launched himself like a sprinter from the lee of the Volvo's boot back across the road. It was an instinctive move to get back on his original track but it was a bad one. A BMW, the driver impatient at the delay, had pulled out from behind the Volvo and was accelerating away, catching, as it did so, the side of Tenison's head as it emerged from behind the Volvo. Even at fifteen miles an hour the impact was enough to crush Tenison's skull.

OCTOBER 16, FRIDAY
VILLACH

She had gone by the time George came down for breakfast. It was a kind of relief. He had not looked forward to saying goodbye to her, had not been able to decide whether to assume his jokey mode or, one last time, to be serious and to say what he thought he thought.

He walked disconsolately along the valley path during the afternoon, the sun if anything warmer than ever – no clichés about the weather matching his mood, he thought. He wondered how long it would be before he began to stop missing her. The problem was that he had no yardstick to go by. He had never felt about anyone like this. It would pass. But he wasn't sure whether he wanted that to happen sooner or later. It was perhaps better to feel seriously sad about someone or something than to feel nothing at all. It was a close thing but, on balance, the pain was a new experience and that just swung it.

He caught the train to Vienna the next day and, picking up the Times at the airport, was satisfied to see SKVP's reply to Alex's final message. He supposed that was the end of it.

In Beirut the next day he took a taxi to the Beau Rivage. He wasn't ready for the rooms at the Commodore yet. Anything might have happened to them; done over by SKVP or the others, ransacked by a marauding sneak-thief or even re-let by his largely-invisible landlord whose speciality was materialising at moments of deepest inconvenience. George's two-month absence, he would explain, broke the tenancy agreement and, thinking that George had left for good, he had had to let it to an Algerian carpet-dealer. Well all that could wait.

In the bar that evening he ordered a bottle of Musar for old times' sake and asked the barman if they still took the London Times. In a moment the man brought him a copy and George slipped him a large note. He turned, sentimentally really, to the back page. He wished he could have done something sloppy like putting in an entry which said "Goodbye chaps, it was fun". It hadn't really been fun, not much of it but, by God it had been different. He had certainly changed. Probably. He had certainly seen and done things of which he had only dreamed – and then inaccurately. He was, there was no doubt about it, sad that it was all over.

He ran his eye down the page. And paused.

Rex.

…he read…

Warm clothing missing. No trace of Q or party.

The girl in red.

LIVERPOOL

Andrew stood at the side of the Aigburth Road, watching the traffic through the driving rain. There was no zebra crossing but he nonetheless irrationally cursed the cars for not stopping to let him pass. He pulled his umbrella down close over his head and, at length, losing patience, stepped out into the flow, zigzagging his way across the two lanes. Behind him a girl in a red mac decided on impulse to follow his example and skipped into the road almost on his left shoulder. As Andrew reached the far pavement he turned left across her, making her pause for a second to avoid a collision. Andrew was never aware of her and Lesley did not recognise him under his umbrella. She turned right and they walked rapidly through the rain away from each other.

About Christopher Kerr

Christopher spent much of his working life in television and the arts. After a spell as director of an arts centre in Liverpool, he joined Granada TV where he worked as a reporter and producer.

Most recently he co-founded Bay TV Liverpool, which, in 2013 won the local broadcast TV franchise for Merseyside.

Now retired, Christopher lives in Wiltshire.